The Non-Stop Connolly Show
Part Three

First published 1978 by Pluto Press Limited
Unit 10 Spencer Court, 7 Chalcot Road, London NW1 8LH

ISBN 0 904383 81 4

Designed by Tom Sullivan
Cover designed by Kate Hepburn
Cover photo: from the London production of
The Non-Stop Connolly Show at the Almost Free Theatre,
by Tom Hutcheson for Inter-Action Limited
Printed in Great Britain by Latimer Trend & Company Ltd Plymouth

Margaretta D'Arcy and John Arden

The Non-Stop Connolly Show
A Dramatic Cycle of Continuous
Struggle in Six Parts

Part Three:
Professional: 1896–1903

Pluto  Plays

To the memory of Liam MacMillen of the Belfast Republican
Clubs, whose vigour and enthusiasm made possible
The Non-Stop Connolly Show in that city: and who was shot
dead in the street only a few days after we had played there.

Margaretta D'Arcy and John Arden

NOTES ON THE AUTHORS:

Margaretta D'Arcy comes from Dublin, where she obtained her early
experience in the theatre. She has worked in the theatre consistently since
1951. Co-author of sixteen scripts for stage, radio and TV. Presently lives in
Galway, where she is involved with experimental community
workshop-theatre. She is currently preparing, with Patricia Cobey, a book
on women in contemporary Ireland to be published by Virago; and her
play *A Pinprick of History*, dealing with the 1977 Irish general election, is
scheduled for production at the Almost Free Theatre.

John Arden was born in Barnsley, Yorkshire. Began full-time theatre
writing in 1958 for the Royal Court, London. Author of *Serjeant
Musgrave's Dance*, *Armstrong's Last Goodnight*, etc. A collection of essays
on the theatre, *To Present The Pretence*, has recently been published by
Eyre Methuen. Forthcoming work includes a radio play, *Pearl*.

AUTHORS' PREFACE

James Connolly holds a unique place in early twentieth-century European history. He was the only revolutionary leader of his time who combined in his career:
- genuine proletarian origins
- a consistent record of work amongst the international socialist movement in several countries (Britain, Ireland, America)
- continuous involvement with trade-union organisations as well as revolutionary political parties
- opposition to the national hysteria of the first world war, which engulfed so much of the international labour-leadership
- practical physical expression of that opposition, in that he was one of the chief organisers of the Dublin Rising of 1916.

Throughout his career, and closely interwoven with each of the above aspects of his life, one can trace the recurrent conflict between *revolution* and *reform* – an ideological dichotomy that still plagues all who have ever had anything to do with left-wing political affairs. In Connolly's case this prolonged debate took on so many shapes and faces that we felt it necessary to explore his experience at deliberately repetitive length – hence a cycle of plays rather than one clean-cut three-act summary. Other recurrent themes that lift their coils in and out of the story, like the serpents' bodies in an old Celtic manuscript-ornament, are:
- the perennial failure of the British Left to recognise and cope with the imperialist role of Britain in relation to Ireland
- the confusion among international socialism caused by the national independence movements in such colonial and semi-colonial countries as Ireland, Poland, Serbia, etc.

These six plays have therefore taken the form of not so much a straight biography of Connolly, as a series of digressive stage-presentations of the events of his time which influenced his political views and consequent actions. They were written to be shown as one complete connected sequence, and have been so produced, both in Dublin and in London. There were certain differences of emphasis between the two productions.

In Dublin our aim was primarily to counteract what one might term the 'Conor Cruise O'Brien historical revisionism', currently much in vogue in Irish intellectual circles, and closely associated with the policies of the Fine Gael-Labour Coalition government – in which Dr Cruise O'Brien was himself a minister. This school of thought appears to maintain:
- that the 1916 Rising was unnecessary
- that Irish Independence would have been achieved anyway through constitutional parliamentary processes
- that the Protestant-Loyalist minority in Ireland (which forms a *majority* in six of the counties of Ulster) is in effect a nation of its own, quite distinct from the rest of the Irish population

– that the present anti-imperialist struggle in the country has therefore no historical validity.

To reinforce these theoretical opinions in the Irish Republic, successive governments (both Fianna Fail and Coalition) have made use of a whole series of repressive measures – including:

    – trials for political offences before a Special Court without a jury

    – official censorship of radio and television broadcasts

    – self-censorship of the press under threat of government interference

    – imprisonment of citizens upon no stronger evidence than the unsupported word of a senior police-officer that he *believes* them to be 'subversives'

    – the 1976 declaration of a State of Emergency to give extra powers to the Army 'in support of the civil authority', and to permit the police to hold persons on suspicion for seven days before bringing them before a court.

Amnesty International has investigated the state of the Irish prisons: and the new Fianna Fail government has been compelled to re-examine the situation. It also appears (5 October 1977) that the seven-day detention system is likely to be shelved, as a result of widespread public disquiet.

The London production of the plays, on the other hand, was intended to demonstrate how the unwillingness of the Labour Movement in Britain to take a firm stand in support of Irish self-determination has resulted throughout several generations in a strengthening of the Anglo-Irish reactionary elements, which in turn has meant the augmentation of violence, bloodshed and widespread public suffering – a process which shows no signs of decrease. This lack of cross-channel awareness and solidarity has been directly responsible for IRA bombings in Britain, with the consequent Prevention of Terrorism Act, the censorship and crypto-censorship of Irish themes in all departments of the British media, the deportation of large numbers of Irish people without adequate means of defence, the maltreatment of Irish political prisoners in British gaols etc. etc . . . The latter point is to be taken up at Strasburg – where the army and police torture-policy in Ulster has already been proven – but the political impact of such revelations upon the broad British Left has, at the time of writing, been negligible.

NOTES ON THE STAGING OF THE PLAYS

Despite the apparent complexity of *The Non-Stop Connolly Show*, its staging need not present any very difficult problems. The approach should be 'emblematic' rather than 'naturalistic'; and ideally a number of stages should be used, arranged around the audience, and connected perhaps with gangways at various levels. We have suggested a series of backcloths which can be fixed either singly or two-at-a-time to give the overall atmosphere of each section of the cycle.

The large cast can be contained by a basic company of about a dozen actors, who will each have to play many different roles, not necessarily of their own sex: but stylised, easily-changed, strongly-defined costumes, and possibly stock-masks for recurrent social types (i.e. bourgeois politicians, employers, military officers, etc.), would greatly assist this technique.

The part of Connolly does not necessarily have to be played by the same actor in all six parts. It might be difficult to find an artist capable of handling him all the way through from childhood to middle-age – but that this taxing feat of character portrayal is possible was proven in Dublin by the remarkable performance of Terry McGinity, who came into the production halfway through rehearsals and became, we are convinced, truly possessed by the dead hero's *daimon*.

The music for the songs in the Dublin and London productions was found from traditional sources—there are many Irish, British and American airs which will fit the words – and we employed an improvised accompaniment, largely percussive, to give accent to the stage movement and the delivery of some of the more rhetorical dialogue and tirade.

The backcloths are described in the text. The style we have in mind should be based on the formal emblematic tradition of trade union banners, and should be carried out in bright colours with no attempt at impressionism or naturalistic representation. The cloths should include appropriate slogans and captions.

Essentially the plays need *speed* – and close attention to *rhythm*. Each scene or episode should be understood as a self-contained combination of voice, movement, colour and music, with a precise dramatic momentum of its own, which makes its point as sharply as possible and is then withdrawn from the stage, as sharply as possible, to be replaced by the next grouping. We would emphasise finally that the play will work only if the actors are more concerned with understanding the political arguments and implications of the story than with 'creating character' in the normal theatrical sense. A few books which could be usefully referred to for this purpose, as well as the works of James Connolly:

C. Desmond Greaves, *The Life and Times of James Connolly*, Lawrence & Wishart.

T. A. Jackson, *Ireland Her Own*, Lawrence & Wishart.

George Dangerfield, *The Strange Death of Liberal England*, MacGibbon & Kee.

Ray Ginger, *Eugene V. Debs*, Collier Books.

Richard M. Watt, *The Kings Depart*, Penguin Books.

James Connolly, *Selected Writings*, ed. by Peter Beresford, Penguin.

Jack Gale, *Oppression and Revolt in Ireland*, Workers' Revolutionary Party Pocket Book No. 15.

The Non-Stop Connolly Show received its first production in Dublin, at Liberty Hall (headquarters of the Irish Transport and General Workers' Union) on Easter weekend, Saturday–Sunday, 29/30 March 1975

Cast

    Connolly Terence J. McGinity

    Larkin Gerry O'Leary

    De Leon Barrie Houghton

Other parts were played by:

Paschal Finnan	Frank Macken
Niamh Fitzgerald	Vincent McCabe
Don Foley	Dave McKenna
Meryl Gourlay	Kevin McKenna
Des Hogan	Fionnuala Rogerson
Boris Howarth	Sandra Rudkin
Margaret Howarth	Paddy Scully
Garret Kehoe	

together with the following members of the Irish Workers' Cultural Centre:

Mildred Fleming	Sheila Moran
Maura Heffernan	Virginia O'Reilly
Paul McGrath	Eamon Walsh
Mick Moran	

Children's parts were played by:

    Members of na Fianna Éireann

    Finn Arden

    Jacob Arden

    Neuss Arden

    During the subsequent tour of the production in Ireland the part of **Connolly** as a boy was played by Neuss Arden.

The direction of the production was co-ordinated by:

    John Arden

    Margaretta D'Arcy

    Jim Sheridan

    Robert Walker

who were also members of the cast.

Others involved in the general administration and preparation of the production:

Senator Michael Mullen and the General Executive Committee ITGWU, Premises Manager and Staff of Liberty Hall, Eoghan Harris, Tom Kilroy, Des Geraghty, Peter Sheridan, Paddy Gillan, Brian Flynn, Tomas Mac Giolla, Mairin de Burca, Tony Ebbes, Bill Whelan, Eric Fleming, Eamonn Travers, Eamonn Smullen, Cathal Goulding, Cathal Og Goulding, Paula, Niall Stokes, Joe Deasy, Margaret Gaj, The Union of Students in Ireland, Jim Nolan, Students Representative Council UCD, Jim Campbell, Des O'Hagan, Bronwen Casson, Norah Lever, Sean Byrne, Raymond Flynn, Felicia McCabe, Ottavio di Fidio . . . and many more.

The production was sponsored by the Irish Transport and General Workers' Union and the Official Sinn Fein Party.

The London presentation of *The Non-Stop Connolly Show* was produced by Inter-action Ltd at the Almost Free Theatre, as a series of rehearsed readings at lunch time, from 17 May–19 June 1976, under the direction of the authors, with a cast recruited in England.

Part Three: Professional 1896–1903

Act One: 'A Movement with some Purpose'. James Connolly becomes a political organiser in Dublin and founds the Irish Socialist Republican Party. He meets the new Ireland of the literary renaissance and disrupts the royal jubilee.

List of characters:

JAMES CONNOLLY
LILLIE CONNOLLY

WILLIAM O'BRIEN
DORMAN
TOM LYNG
JACK LYNG

Trade-Union ORGANISER
Independent Labour Party CANVASSER

3 WORKERS, one a young woman

NATIONALIST QUESTIONER
UNIONIST QUESTIONER
FABIAN QUESTIONER
PURE SOCIALIST QUESTIONER

MAUD GONNE
W. B. YEATS
ALICE MILLIGAN
ERNEST MILLIGAN

GRABITALL
3 EMPLOYERS
MAGISTRATE
POLICE CONSTABLE

A STRIKER, Leader of a strike picket
Local Government OFFICIAL
LIBRARY ATTENDANT
workers, strikers, unemployed, beggars, police, citizens, etc.

Act Two: 'Alarums and Excursions'. James Connolly, in Dublin, leads the Irish Socialist Republican Party in militant opposition to British imperialism and the Boer War. He is criticised by Keir Hardie of the British labour movement.

List of characters:

JAMES CONNOLLY

WILLIAM O'BRIEN
TOM LYNG
JACK LYNG
ALICE MILLIGAN
ERNEST MILLIGAN
STEWART

MAUD GONNE
W. B. YEATS

GRABITALL
3 EMPLOYERS
CIVIL SERVANT
JOE DEVLIN
ORANGEMAN
PRIEST

POLICE OFFICER
JUDGE

AFRICAN BEARER
BOER
GERMAN ARMS MERCHANT
FRENCH ARMS MERCHANT

PRIME MINISTER
2 Liberal MPs

KEIR HARDIE
BERNARD SHAW
BEATRICE WEBB
SYDNEY WEBB
ARTHUR GRIFFITH
  citizens, demonstrators, police, Members of Parliament, etc.

Act Three: 'Outmanoeuvred'. James Connolly is rejoiced to find the Irish Socialist Republican Party recognised by the Socialist International. Rosa Luxemburg – in controversy with Kautsky – throws doubt upon Connolly's views of Irish nationhood. The ISRP throws doubt upon his views of political priorities. He determines to go elsewhere.

List of characters:

JAMES CONNOLLY
LILLIE CONNOLLY
NORA CONNOLLY (their daughter)

Mr RIORDAN (their neighbour)
OLD MARKET-WOMAN
BEGGING CHILD

WILLIAM O'BRIEN
TOM LYNG
JACK LYNG
STEWART
BRADSHAWE

GRABITALL
1st and 3rd EMPLOYERS
PRIEST

CHAIRMAN of International Socialist Conference
ROSA LUXEMBURG
KAUTSKY
2 French DELEGATES
2 Polish DELEGATES
Bulgarian DELEGATE

American Railway CONDUCTOR
Chorus of American TRAVELLERS
Socialist Conference DELEGATES

Part Three: Professional 1896–1903

ACT 1: 'A Movement with some Purpose'

SCENE 1

A bird's-eye view of Dublin around its bay, with the Georgian buildings rearing up amongst the slums. The whole guarded by redcoat soldiers and police. (Back-cloth 3.)

Enter GRABITALL. CONNOLLY *and* LILLIE *enter with baggage and children. There are beggars pestering all passers-by.*

Grabitall Mona and Nora and Aideen and Lillie and James—
      Yes, three children now – no doubt very soon there'll be four –
      Improvident as always – it's not *me* puts the wolf at their door –
      They pack up their poor luggage and travel by boat and by train
      From Scotland to Ireland, from a country of hunger and cold
      To a country of cold and of hunger as indeed might have well
        been foretold.
      This man has not come here to work
      And keep his wretched family – no mistake:
      He's come to spout and agitate,
      Declare, demand, all in a heat
      Disturb the apathetic peace
      Which, since the death of turbulent Charles Parnell
      And since the last defeat of Gladstone's Liberal power,
      Chokes the united voice that thundered for Home Rule.
      Lord Salisbury's Tory Government has a plan –
      Lest separatism, independent aspirations, once again
      Rear up their strength and break the empire's bond,
      Coercion now is done with: we are *kind* . . .
      More liberal than the Liberals – we will grant
      Reform of land, local elections; oh we will freely plant
      Hope of commercial growth to stultify
      All racial disaffection amongst the middle class.
      The anarchic rumble of the ignorant mob will pass
      Into oblivion – trade unions and the Labour Party, dust in a
       half-blind eye,
      Are both controlled from Britain and therefore pose no threat.
      For complete imperial unity we have achieved the best chance yet!

      Mr Crookey, Mr O'Hookey – where's O'Toole?

Enter 1ST, 2ND *and* 3RD EMPLOYERS.

Chorus, gentlemen, please!

Employers (*singing*)

> We will now encourage and cause to flourish
> The native knowledge of our ancient land!

3rd Employer

> I'm setting up a factory for the baking of biscuits and bread.

1st Employer

> I'm setting up another one for the making of boxes of wood
> For the package and storage of biscuits and bread.

2nd Employer

> I'm setting up an all-Ireland transport concern
> For the conveyance of Hibernian boxes of wood
> Full of native-baked Gaelic biscuits and bread
> To all parts of the country be canal and be road and be train –

1st Employer We need men –

3rd Employer We need women –

2nd Employer We need men –

Employers

> Because of British domination
> Upon the trade of our poor nation –

Grabitall Ssh – you don't mention Home Rule! You forget yourselves, gentlemen!

Employers Ssh – ssh – we forgot ourselves . . . But Mr Grabitall, nonetheless, sorr . . .

> Because of *da-da* domination
> Upon the trade of our poor *da-da*,
> Creating ruinous competition
> We're put into the sad position –

1st Employer Of having to say to every man we hire –

3rd Employer The wage is small, we can give you no more!

Exit GRABITALL, *with a patronising pat on their backs.*
UNEMPLOYED WORKERS *enter.*

2nd Employer Take it or leave it, do you refuse the job?

1st Worker

> Sure between this and Ballydehob
> There is no other work that I can find.
> I have a mind
> To go to England and do better there.

3rd Employer

> So go! Where you come from there's plenty more. Next!

2nd Worker

> My farm has failed. My family are poor.
> I'll work for what you give me and endure.

1st Employer
> You have your grateful patriotic reasons? Good.

2nd Worker
> I can't afford the fare
> Across the water. I want food.

3rd Employer
> And food for Irish bellies in my factory is produced.
> Young woman, you were all but seduced
> Into the British brothels, were you not? Come, work for me
> And live your frugal life in catholic purity!

3rd Worker (*a young woman*)
> From worse than death they rescued me indeed –
> Jasus, for all my lifetime do I need
> To look for rescue day after bloody day?
> I'd rather have a decent rate of pay . . .
> Maybe I should be careful what I say . . .

Employers Come work work work . . .!

Those who have obtained employment begin working very hard to a fast rhythm clapped out by the EMPLOYERS. *The others stand around in a weary group.*

SCENE 2

Enter DORMAN *with his leaflets and a placard clearly printed 'The Socialist Answer' – not very successful in getting anyone to take them. A* TRADE UNION ORGANISER *bounces in.*

TU Organiser
> There are, you know, trade unions:
> We cannot help you all at once –
> But for craftsmen, tradesmen, carpenters, engineers,
> Solidarity and combined action will relieve so many fears.
> Pay a subscription, take a card:
> Remember, we must push hard
> If our British parent-body is eventually to agree
> That we too have an important voice
> In their counsels from beyond the sea.
> Of course, if your work is labouring, casual, unskilled,
> We have no place in our congress where your hopes may be
>   fulfilled.

Those working turn away from him, disappointed. He speaks to DORMAN:

> And of course, if your main interest is political agitation,
> We regret we are not prepared to discuss the state of the nation:

> In due time, very possibly, but at the moment we must say to you
> It is not very wise to bite more than you can chew . . .!

Exit TU ORGANISER.

Employers (*still clap the time*)
> Work work work . . .!

They lead their WORKERS *out.*

Unemployed Worker
> And they do work until each arm and leg
> Buckles and cracks. They are the fortunate.
> For us: sure we can emigrate
> Or tout for short odd jobs upon the corner of the street,
> Or, failing both of these, hold out our hand and beg.

Enter Independent Labour Party CANVASSER, *with a placard and leaflets*

ILP Canvasser
> The Independent Labour Party, responsive to the bould Keir
>   Hardie,
> Looks for votes in the election to the Dublin City Corporation.
> We hope next year beyond in Belfast
> Our men will sit on the council at last!
> For water, gas, and sewage disposal
> We have many and many a brave proposal –

Dorman Socialism . . .?

ILP Canvasser Now don't let's try to run until we can learn to walk . . .

Exit ILP CANVASSER. *One of the* UNEMPLOYED, *begging, approaches* DOR-
MAN.

Dorman (*gives him a small coin*) I shouldn't really be doing this, you know. It won't help, you know. Socialism . . .! Have a leaflet.

Connolly (*approaches* DORMAN) Excuse me – I'm looking for the Dublin Socialist Club, can you tell me where it is?

Dorman Yes: in point of fact: here.

Connolly Here?

Dorman Yes, myself. Me. I'm practically the only member at the moment, I'm afraid. Can I help you?

Connolly My name is Connolly.

Dorman How d'you do? What can I do for you? Would you care for one of our leaflets . . . good heavens! Connolly! From Edinburgh! James Connolly! Oh dear me, I'm so sorry, Mr Connolly, you quite took me by surprise. Did you have a good trip? Why don't we go to the club-room – oh we do have a club-room, despite all appearances – my name, by the way, is Dorman. I'm so glad you've been able to come – this way, Mr Connolly, through the door marked *Public Bar*, we *call* it our club-room, though really it's only the snug, the landlord lets us use it on Tuesdays and Thursdays . . .

Lillie (*catches on to Connolly*) James, I am not bringing the children into any public bar. There's a notice over there that says there's a room to let. I'll go straight across and see about it. Come on, girls, come on . . . I suppose I had better look out for some washing or sewing to take in . . .

She takes the CHILDREN *out one way, and* DORMAN, *leading* CONNOLLY *out the other, brings him straight back again as though into the club-room. They are joined by the members of the club.*

SCENE 3

O'BRIEN, TOM LYNG, JACK LYNG *sit down.* DORMAN *introduces* CONNOLLY *to them.* (O'BRIEN *has a limp and walks with a stick throughout.*)

Dorman We meet in the snug of a pub, though most of us prefer to
      abstain:
      We find it difficult for all of us to be together at any one time:
      We are, as I said, very few: the brothers Lyng, William O'Brien –
      Mr Connolly has come as invited, to endeavour to sort us all out –
      Here he is, brimming over with fruitful suggestions: no doubt . . .!
Connolly The first remark I have to make
      Brings a blush into my cheek:
      But had we not best start as we mean to go on –
      What sort of wage can I expect to earn?
      The fact is, I can't imagine –
      However large your subscription –
      This club is in any way capable
      Of employing a full-time official?
      To do what work,
      For how many days each week?
      What facilities, what expenses, and basically for what hope?
      This is a matter before which nothing else can be disposed:
      As you know, I have a family to feed and house and clothe.
Dorman Good. Well: that's candid. Vice versa, why not?
Tom Lyng We are a very small club –
Jack Lyng Not even a club –
Dorman A collection –
Tom Lyng Of all manner of individuals, all loosely devoted to the general
      principles
Jack Lyng Of socialism –
Dorman Right! But our activities –
Tom Lyng Amount to practically nothing –
Jack Lyng Except a meeting once a week on the steps of the Custom House –
Dorman To which hardly anybody comes – and of course we issue leaflets –
Connolly D'you get them out yourselves?

Tom Lyng No. They're printed in England by various fraternal groups.

Jack Lyng So we haven't got much money.

Dorman We could pay you a regular wage or on a job-by-job basis, or out-of-pocket expenses –

Connolly It'll amount to no great income if all I have to do is the kind of thing you're already doing.

Tom Lyng We don't want you to do that.

Jack Lyng We would like you, if you can, with all your experience from Scotland –

Dorman To transform us, if that is possible, into a movement with some purpose . . .

Connolly Purpose . . . It means what? I will tell you what it means. It means a properly organised revolutionary party – nothing less, or I am done with it. And the concomitants are as follows: regular subscriptions, a weekly or a monthly newspaper, a permanent working committee, a rank-and-file membership that is actually prepared to do some work when it is wanted and, of course, a manifesto. We get together an ad hoc working-party, we can draw one up without delay: and we can take the opportunity of exploring each other's political views – right? Then we present the manifesto to a general meeting of the entire club, any friends, any sympathisers, invite them all in, from Dublin, Cork, Belfast – throw it open to the widest controversy! And already we have made a name!

They all huddle together as a working-party with their backs to the audience – except O'BRIEN *– who comes downstage to speak.*

O'Brien Before they fetched him over here they were talking about him continually – Connolly will say so-and-so, his point of view will be this and that – I asked, who was this Connolly? 'He's a very smart fellow', I was told. 'And what is he?' 'Just a labourer.' 'A labourer?' said I, 'How could a labourer know all these things?' 'He went to the Library in Edinburgh and he studied.' This was not very convincing to me. I could not understand how a labourer should be so important as all that. The labourers I am acquainted with are people who drift around the roads and take up casual jobs and are almost entirely illiterate. However, I had to accept what was stated . . .

And here today I see this labouring man stand up and take
His tablets to the multitude like Moses on the rock . . .

SCENE 4

The CLUB-MEMBERS *take their seats as though on the platform of a public meeting,* CONNOLLY *in the middle. He holds the manifesto.*

Connolly The announcement of the formation of a new revolutionary party.

Which calls for the establishment of an Irish socialist republic. Which will be based upon the public ownership of the land and of all instruments of production, distribution and exchange. Which demands the nationalisation, under the control of properly elected boards, of both agriculture and industry, a minimum wage and a forty-eight-hour week, free education under the control of popularly elected committees, pensions to be paid for out of a graduated income-tax: and universal suffrage. The party to be known as the Irish Socialist Republican Party. In accordance with our belief that the subjection of one nation to another, as of Ireland to the authority of the British crown, is a barrier to the free political and economic development of the subjected nation, and can only serve the interests of the exploiting classes of both nations. We want to set up branches everywhere. The minimum weekly subscription is one penny per member, and the entrance fee is sixpence. A weekly newspaper to be known as *The Workers' Republic* will be published as soon as our financial circumstances allow. Any questions?

Questions come from the floor of the house:

Nationalist Questioner Does not the Catholic Church teach that private property is ordained of God?

Connolly The private property of the money-changers who were driven out of the temple – what does the church teach as to the rights and wrongs of that?

Nationalist Questioner The socialist ideology is alien to the Gaelic race.

Connolly And what d'you think St Patrick brought here but an alien ideology? Why, you argue like a pagan druid! And moreover from the same premises – the ultimate identity of church and state.

Exit NATIONALIST QUESTIONER.

And there you see the potentiality of your middle-class revolution. Oh they will talk until the moon turns green about freedom for the people – but the moment they feel their own property is threatened, they will abandon you and run, crying out on the name of God. Next?

Unionist Questioner The beginning of social revolution in Europe was the protestant reformation of the sixteenth century: the trade union movement of Great Britain is the legitimate inheritor of the puritan conventicles of the seventeenth century: and only by securing ourselves firmly to that movement can labour organisations in Ireland expect and enjoy the solidarity they require. Republicanism is a red herring.

Exit UNIONIST QUESTIONER.

Connolly And there ye see the potentiality of your unionist revolution. Defensive and sectarian: and in the end amalgamated with the Tory bosses of the City of London. Next?

Fabian Questioner Excuse me: I was most impressed with the general grasp of political reality conveyed in your programme: but I wonder, as a stranger from England, if you have altogether appreciated the *abrupt* nature of the reforms you have so sensibly outlined? Would it not be possible to reach equally desirable goals by means of evolution rather than revolution? By permeating, perhaps, the existing democratic structures, upon a long-term electoral strategy: and by laying for the time being more emphasis upon, say, your schools project, rather than upon the more divisive political theme of a republic?

Connolly If reform was all we wanted, we could get it, from Lord Salisbury, by means, as you say, of the existing democratic structures. He has a man over here already, in Dublin Castle, paying bribes to the Irish people in the shape of school projects and other such-like benefits, exactly for the purpose of preventing revolution and encouraging evolution. And making sure that evolution will in the long run never be socialist.

Fabian Questioner Yes I suppose so . . . I do think, however, you ought not to condemn the existing administration without a thorough grasp of the statistics involved. The whole question of getting rid of the hidebound capitalist-bureaucratic system can only be undertaken with extensive research, and – dare I say it – *experience* in the ramifications of local government? Thank you so much.

Exit FABIAN QUESTIONER.

Connolly Aye: the potentiality of your fabian revolution. Experience and research in the existing hidebound system till no-one can tell whether 'tis you or the system are bound up with the strongest hide! Next.

Pure Socialist Questioner I would, as a convinced atheist and internationalist of long standing, put these points to the speaker, as follows, viz: we start with materialism . . . and thus, dialectically, arrive at revolution. Karl Marx has made abundantly clear the impossibility of revolution in primarily peasant economies such as Russia – and therefore, by extension, Ireland . . .

Connolly And your question?

Pure Socialist Questioner Question? Oh yes . . . you are premature. In this country, it can't be done.

Connolly But your question?

Pure Socialist Questioner Well: I mean – can it? The very existence of this new party is simply playing into the hands of the imperialist, chauvinist, capitalist cliques: comrade, let me tell you, if you want a revolution you've got to sit down and bloody *plan* for it. You can't just write it out on a little bit of paper and expect us to take it on trust . . .

Exit PURE SOCIALIST QUESTIONER.

Connolly Do I really need to sum up the purist revolution? All theory and damn-all else. Thank you very much.

The meeting breaks up.

Well –
>The brambles and the briars are clean cleared away and cut:
>The green of the young tree will drink up life from every root.

Tom Lyng We have a membership of eight.

Enter GRABITALL.

Connolly We will soon get more than that.
O'Brien Oh we won't if we stay here:
>We must work, we must go out –

Connolly (*to* O'BRIEN)
>I saw your eyelid on the droop –
>You experienced some short doubt?
>Does it bother you yet?

O'Brien It does not.
>I am quite sure.
>When I see the class of man that your words have turned away
>I am convinced absolutely that yours is the straightest way.

Connolly So we go out and we do it.
>We are young enough and strong enough to lose nothing if we
>>attempt it.
>The small clear statement – if indeed it be correct –
>By being so small has no choice but to talk direct.

Grabitall Direct small speech in this cantankerous noisy town
>Nine times out of ten is not heard or is shouted down.
>Drink from a thousand taprooms ends up down the drain,
>Urine and vomit drag each Dublin dream
>In sodden fragments to the Liffey's brim –
>Against this tide who strives but bold undaunted Jim?
>How long before he finds he has not yet learned how to swim . . . ?

SCENE 5

CONNOLLY *becomes aware of some difficulty engaging the members of the* ISRP. *He looks inquiringly at* DORMAN.

Dorman The subscriptions to the new party should easily have provided
>One pound for you per week after all expenses divided –

Connolly But they don't?
Dorman Dear me, they do not.
O'Brien D'you see, we were expecting the great part of our rank-and-file support to be from the lads in the building-trade: but they're all out on strike.
Tom Lyng It's not apathy, it's bloody poverty.
Connolly So don't insist on subscriptions. Chalk 'em up and let 'em in. We are not making a business out of this business, d'ye get me?

O'Brien But where does that leave *you*? Sure the first question you put to us was how much you would get paid.

CONNOLLY *shrugs. The* ISRP MEMBERS *leave him.*

Connolly Was I not wise when I was a young man
       Neither to drink nor smoke, for now I find
       Just so much money in my hand
       As will keep me and mine for just one week.
       Seven days therefore I have to look for work.

The EMPLOYERS *enter, each with a placard reading 'Situations Vacant'. During the song,* CONNOLLY *approaches them one by one to ask for work, but each time the placard is turned round and he reads the inscription on the reverse: 'No Vacancies'. This becomes a kind of* danse macabre, *the* EMPLOYERS *enticing him on deliberately to enjoy his disappointment.*

Grabitall (*sings*)
       There is no doubt that even though
       The trade of Dublin is depressed
       If confidence can be maintained
       All things will turn out for the best.
Employers (*sing*)
       We have no work for you any more
       That sign should be taken off the door.
Grabitall (*sings*)
       America, I grieve to say,
       Across the ocean starts to pose
       A serious threat to world-wide trade:
       Some British firms may have to close.
Employers (*sing*)
       We have no work for you any more
       That sign should be taken off the door.
Grabitall (*sings*)
       And in the German empire steel
       Is being produced at such a speed
       Unless there is an enormous war
       For Sheffield there'll be no more need.
Employers (*sing*)
       We have no work for you any more
       That sign should be taken off the door.
Grabitall (*sings*)
       Therefore it is incumbent on
       All Dublin men to show restraint
       In wage demands at such a time –
       I will not hear your cheap complaint!

Employers (*sing*)
>We have no work for you any more
>That sign should be taken off the door.

Enter BUILDING STRIKERS *on picket*.

Grabitall I address myself particularly to the members of the building-trade
(*Sings*) How can you think that we can spend
>Unheard-of sums on brick and stone
>When in productive industry
>Our profits hardly hold their own?
Employers (*sing*)
>We have no work for you any more
>That sign should be taken off the door!
Grabitall And I tell you if this strike goes on
>There'll be no work for anyone ever again!

Exeunt GRABITALL *and* EMPLOYERS.

SCENE 6

Re-enter 3RD EMPLOYER (*as Nationalist MP*).

A Striker And here comes our member of parliament, me boys, to support
us in our strike! Three cheers and a rouser for the party of Parnell!
3rd Employer (*acknowledges the cheers*) Now look here, men, I have to tell
you you are grievously misled. This strike is an anti-national strike, it is
fomented in the interests of British big business and it has no other purpose than to bring the Irish economy down upon its bleeding knees!
You must all go back to work.

Exit 3RD EMPLOYER.

Striker Jasus – is that what we voted for!
Connolly (*comes up to picket*) On behalf of the Irish Socialist Republican
Party I have a formal proposition to put to you.
Striker What? Who are you? Aren't you the feller was round this morning
spying out for a job of work?
Connolly My suggestion is this: the Dublin Trades Council and the ISRP set
up a joint committee to put forward a candidate for that waster's con-
stituency the very next election. A Labour candidate. It can be done.
Striker It's not on.
Connolly Why not?
Striker Premature. We don't know you. Oh yes, we've read your leaflets.
We've also heard that seven-eighths of the active trade unionists in
Dublin walked out of your first meeting.

CONNOLLY *turns away, disappointed.*

Hey – brother – about that question of a job you were looking for: corporation new drainage scheme – they want all manner of unskilled labour – but bring your own shovel and I'd recommend you to put the word out for some waterproof clothing . . .

Exeunt STRIKERS.

SCENE 7

Connolly I will knock once more
  Upon this final door –
  To the Dublin Corporation
  I put in my application
  For an unskilled situation
  Digging drains for sanitation . . .

He knocks and an OFFICIAL *appears.*

Official The relevant department
  Regrets to have to say
  That its progressive drainage project
  Is subject to delay –
  Due to, as the public
  Officially have been told,
  Untoward technical circumstances
  Outside of our control:
  Due to, as in private
  Unofficially I can make it known,
  Bureaucratic obstruction
  That has clogged its way down
  From the government in Westminster
  To Dublin Castle and the City Hall:
  We will never get this town cleaned up
  Until we get Home Rule.
Connolly No, no, that's a delusion. Can I give you a leaflet? The ISRP holds meetings outside the Custom House every Saturday afternoon and on Sunday evenings, and Tuesdays at – –
Official Here – I'm a civil servant! D'you want to put the heart across me with the likes of that handbill! Unemployed labourers advocating a godless republic!
Connolly Is there a chance of a job or isn't there?
Official Indeed there is not. Merciful hour, whatever next . . .!

Exit OFFICIAL.

Connolly Whatever next, there is no question now
      The state we live in is a monarchy indeed.
      Our sovereign ruler wears a threefold crown:
      The three brass balls above the pawnshop door . . .

    Enter o'BRIEN.

O'Brien Jim – ! Did ye hear, the building strike is over!
Connolly And who won?
O'Brien The carpenters have settled without consulting the labourers. The labourers have disaffiliated from the trades council in consequence. Proletarian solidarity comes home from the pump like water in a sieve.
Connolly We'll get out a leaflet.
O'Brien I thought we should call a meeting. This time we may be able to collect a few subscriptions? Sure the labourers are bound to be bloody livid at the whole business – their situation at this moment is not one to be envied – –
Connolly Oh yes it is.
O'Brien Jesus-and-Mary: I forgot it altogether . . . the work on the drainage is beginning at last.
Connolly They have me marked as a trouble-maker.
O'Brien Well: you have been observed in and out of the library, round the bookstalls on the quay . . . which does mean you make trouble. But it also means this: the foreman's been forewarned that if he doesn't treat ye decent ye'll write him up every word in your forthcoming encyclopedia – the foreman's an ould butty of an ould butty of a friend of mine – so get hold of some waterproof gear. Five o'clock tomorrow morning . . .

    Exit o'BRIEN.

SCENE 8

    Enter LILLIE.

Lillie Oh James, I am so glad, so glad, after all this long time! I must brush up your clothes and you must mend your shoes tonight. I have a bit of leather put by for you but you looked so tired I didn't mention it.
Connolly Aye, I was tired: but you know, I don't believe I shall ever be tired again! To have no work is more exhausting than the hardest labour in all the world. So where's the leather . . .? And let's hope I make a better fist of it than I did in Edinburgh, hey?

    He sits down and starts mending his shoes. LILLIE *looks after his coat.*

    Oh my God . . .!
Lillie What's the matter?
Connolly My boots. I've just ruined them. The wet today has made them rotten

and will you look at them – I've pulled them apart! I can't dig a drain without boots.

Lillie Oh, James – now let me think. You have your slippers. They've got good strong soles, and the top comes right up to your trousers – if they could be tied with a bit of string – here –

She adjusts his slippers for him.

Do you think you could manage with these for one day? We could buy you a second-hand pair of boots in the morning – sure won't we be able to afford them now you've got work? You could do with the slippers for one day, couldn't you, James – couldn't you?

Connolly Aye, aye: they have strong soles. And the trousers hide the string. Why, surely, unless I was to work in a ten-foot pit of mud, you couldn't find a better pair from Glasnevin to Deansgrange. They'll do – by God we'll make them do!

Exit CONNOLLY.

Enter GRABITALL.

Grabitall It was not in a ten-foot pit of mud
But one so deep that even with a rod
You could not measure it in the pouring rain.
And here your bold man has to work from five a.m. till nine
O'clock at night. His humble home
Awaits him in an apprehensive gloom . . .

Exit GRABITALL.

LILLIE *paces about anxiously. The clock strikes ten.*
CONNOLLY *staggers in, absolutely dead-beat.*

Connolly (*sits down*) It's all right . . . It's all right, Lillie . . .

Lillie Oh James, my poor James . . . don't try to eat anything. Drink this, it will do you good.

Connolly I haven't the strength, Lillie, I haven't the strength . . .

He pushes the tea away.

Oh God, Lillie, I'm no good. I'm no use to you and the children. The wheelbarrows, all day: cement in the big barrows: all day long and nothing else. I'm no use to you and the children. I cannot do the work! And as for the revolution . . . ! Oh James Connolly will *talk* the strongest man in all of Dublin into the deepest hole was ever dug! Lillie, I disgust myself.

Lillie After months of starvation, how *could* they expect you – sure, disgust is the right word: but I wouldn't stick it on *you.*

She puts his feet in warm water, eases his braces, etc.

Now, James, you are to rest there till I come back from a message . . .

She slips out.

Connolly (*to audience*)
> The work I do for all of *you*
> Will not be done in time
> Unless I find
> Some other way to do the work
> I do for those within my home . . .
> How many lives can I keep living,
> And how much life can I continue giving?
> I thought, when I came home tonight I'd read a book:
> But every letter in the book is running from me
> Like the pull of a flooded brook –
> The waves of words float hopelessly in and out of my skull –
> How strange I have had no patience ever
> With any man that I thought was a fool . . .

LILLIE *re-enters.*

Lillie (*softly – he is too tired to turn round to her*) James . . . James . . . You need not go back again to be killed again tomorrow.

She shows him money.

Connolly Where did you get this? Where'd you get it, Lillie? Lillie. Lillie!

Lillie Sure 'twas only my little gold watch. Didn't you give it me in Edinburgh – I couldn't bear to part with it! But just now when I saw how you were – James, for the first time ever you were losing your faith in yourself: I knew it would have to go.

Connolly I'll make it up to you, Lillie. God help me, I'll make it up to you. The very first thing in the morning, I'll – –

Lillie You'd do better to stay in bed.

Connolly No. I must go to the National Library. I know well it's not *work*. Book-reading, that's all: and bought for, minute by minute, at the cost of your gold watch. But it's work. I've got to do it.

Exit LILLIE.

SCENE 9

Connolly (*sings*)
> Every day in the National Library
> The same book I take out of the shelf
> In no bookshop have I ever found it
> Heard its name upon nobody's mouth.
>
> Half-a-century since it was written
> By a cripple, a feeble poor man

Who in prison did die of a blood-bursting lung:
If he hadn't, no doubt he'd have hanged.

If they'd hanged him a national martyr,
Unbounded his glory and fame –
But writing a book for this people is not
Any way to preserve your good name.

Yet he wrote it and here I have found it
I copy it out slow and sure –
James Fintan Lalor, *The Faith of a Felon*:
I will shout it in each Irish ear – !

At all events, whisper it . . .

Copy it out and make sure it is printed
Pass it on then from hand to poor hand –
Let it not be forgot, before Marx grew his beard
Fintan Lalor put forth this demand –

'The entire soil of a country belongs of right to the people of that country.
To be let to whom they will. On condition that the tenant shall owe no
allegiance whatsoever to any prince, power, or people – other than those
of the nation whose lands he is permitted to hold . . .' Which means that
the unionist landlords in Ireland, and the unionist administration in
Dublin Castle which supports them, have defaulted in their obligations to
their *own* proper landlords. That's *us*! And we, being thus defrauded,
have no alternative but to evict!

My Lord Lieutenant, are you there?
Here's Captain Blazer before your door.
You are ordered by the Irish people this very day
To vacate your rented premises without hindrance or delay.
Queen Victoria, do you hear?
Or do we have to break the door?
Distasteful but it must be done:
Cathleen ni Houlihaun, break it down . . .!

Who dares to stand and tell me that republicanism and socialism are in
no way compatible!

In the academic exactitude of this funereal reading-room
The lie has been refuted: the truth at last comes home!

LIBRARY ATTENDANT *slides up to him.*

Library Attendant Ssh, you are disturbing Madame Maud Gonne . . .

MAUD GONNE *comes over to* CONNOLLY *and looks at the book he is holding.*

Maud Gonne You are not only reading him – you are copying him out.

Connolly I am so sorry – did I distract you?

Maud Gonne The point about Lalor is this: nothing in the rural areas has changed since he wrote that book. Do you realise that in the western counties at this moment there is the onset of a potato-famine nearly as bad as eighteen forty-seven? Oh, I know who you are – you are the red Scotchman from Dundee.

Connolly Edinburgh. And I'm Irish.

Maud Gonne Keir Hardie told me about you.

Connolly Keir Hardie – you know him?

Maud Gonne I don't know him, but I've met him. He wanted me to pull his chestnuts out of the fire for him in London. He said the socialists of Britain ought not to allow the Famine Queen to be given sixty years of jubilee through the streets of her capital when there were poor men and women starving within a mile of Buckingham Palace, and the strikes, and the unemployment, *et patati et patata* . . . and would I help? *Et par consequence, je lui ai dit*: if the socialists of Britain are going to prevent it, let them do so, why ask me? *Je suis Irlandaise, bien sûr* . . . Oh I knew what he had in mind – if anything should go wrong, like a riot in Trafalgar Square, one or two men dead perhaps from the cudgels of the police – there would be no-one to blame for it but a wild woman from the Celtic west whose inflammatory speech had passed all the bounds of proper British convention. If I am to resist the jubilee, here is where I do it. For the sake of Sligo and Mayo and Galway – before Pimlico. Do you know that this happened in Cahirciveen, this year: a widow-woman, her rent six-pound-twelve-and-six upon her one small field, she lifted but three baskets of potatoes, all worthless as food or as seed. Her only other income: the butter she would churn herself – six pounds in the whole year. Her landlord demanded rent, let her pay or he would evict. She gave him the money. It was everything she had. Everything. What will she do now? What will they all do?

Connolly America?

Maud Gonne Where the speculators and the Tammany politicians tell them lie upon lie – they want them there for one reason –

Connolly That they work for small wages, they know nothing about trade unions, and any crook that can once get them in to the country has their vote for evermore. Dublin Castle forbye is as glad to have them go as the Americans are to receive them. Well, some of the Americans.

Maud Gonne Certainly not those who are put out of work by their arrival. *Mais c'est correcte, la verité*. Did you know famine-fever has broken out at Crossmolina? I have been there, I have seen it. I have myself, alone, confronted the Board of Guardians in the town of Belmullet and demanded that they issue some relief to the poor people – of whom at least ten thousand stood behind me in the street – I was wearing, *par chance, par bonne chance*, my robe and cloak of green. An old man at the back cried out in Irish – 'She is the Queen of the Shee come to Mayo to save the people!' – the Shee, you know who I mean, they live secretly under the hills –

Connolly You mean they thought you were a *fairy* – ? Oh, come now –

Maud Gonne It was convenient for them to tell each other they thought I was a fairy. For how else would they have found the courage to defy the armed police? At all events they did so. They got what they cried out for. Six shillings per week. Seed potatoes from Scotland at the government expense. I told them: 'You have won these things by your numbers, your united strength. By your strength and your courage you must win the freedom of Ireland.' But I am not sure they followed me quite so far as that ... Will you help me create in the city of Dublin a Queen Victoria's jubilee beyond all jubilees that were ever thought of?

Connolly If the Queen of the Shee indeed were to have come from under her green hill,

> She could not with greater speed subject me to her will.
> May I tell you: I've not been well?
> I'm in no state for the sudden glamourie
> Of the silver voice of a well-dressed lady ...
> Will I dispel it with a charm?
> I hold it up so, between finger and thumb.

He moves away from her, holds up his hand towards her, with thumb and forefinger crooked, and speaks very rapidly and aggressively.

Understand the reality of soundly principled class struggle. Unite British and Irish workers. Recognise capitalist nature of exploitation. Unmask both monarchical and nationalist mysticism. Identify the enemy, identify the enemy, identify the enemy upon lines of correct analysis. Strengthen the position of the Irish Socialist Republican Party ... Can I interest you, while we're at it, in becoming a member? Now you can't go answering *that* with a kind of deceptive poetry.

Maud Gonne I hope not.

Connolly Oh: you don't like poetry?

Maud Gonne Potatoes are what matter.

Connolly My God, yes: but from what I had heard of you I would not have thought –

Maud Gonne

> That *I* would have said so?
> Lalor wrote a book, he fell sick, he fell dead.
> They should not look at *me* until that book has been read.

She takes CONNOLLY *and leads him round the stage.*

The most beautiful woman in the whole of Dublin city

Takes hold of the short squat labouring man and brings him in
to her committee . . .

SCENE 10

Maud Gonne Willie – !

Enter YEATS, *followed by* MILLIGAN *and* ALICE MILLIGAN. *She introduces
them to* CONNOLLY.

W. B. Yeats, the greatest poet in the English tongue:
Though this is not yet known, he is still too young.
Alice Milligan and her brother from the sour town of Belfast:
She publishes a political paper and he is confused and lost
Among the myth and legend of the ancient Gael.

Milligan We the Irish will be fighting for ever and ever again we faint and
fail . . .

Yeats I hear the shadowy horses, their long manes a-shake
  Their hoofs heavy with tumult, their eyes glimmering white –
We have proposed, that in order to counteract the philistine jingoism of
Queen Victoria's jubilee, we should set afoot copious and nation-wide
celebrations of the centenary of the rebellion of seventeen ninety-eight . . .

Connolly Very good, that's for *next* year. But by then the Queen's jubilee will
have made its effect. If the organisers for that event do succeed in whip-
ping up more enthusiasm for the monarchy than has been known here for
years – how will you manage in twelve months to reconvert the population towards a bunch of defeated rebels?

Yeats We have proposed – –

Alice Milligan Mr Yeats has proposed – –

Yeats Shouldn't we take it as a committee-decision, Miss Milligan? I prefer
the associative *we* –

Milligan Conveniently ambiguous: could be confused with a speech from the
throne . . .

Yeats We have proposed that this committee should take part in the jubilee
too: but in order to *mourn* the event rather than *celebrate*.

Maud Gonne (*to* CONNOLLY) Will you help?

Connolly (*to audience*)
  You will tell me these are no socialists, you will tell me I should
    not join
  With the idealistic middle classes: they will drop away from us
    one by one – ?
  We have a membership of *eight*! The pale hand of the English
    Queen
  Plasters over the whole of Ireland with comp lacency and deceit:

> I will join my voice with anyone who has the spirit to cry out
> And say: NO – we are alone
> We are Irish and our own men!
> We must be heard, we must be seen
> And we must not be forgotten.

Make your plans: I'll go along with them. And the ISRP will be proud to participate.

Alice Milligan (*takes* CONNOLLY *aside*) Anything you want to write about Lalor, Mr Connolly, I'll publish in my paper.

Connolly It's understood there'll be no poetry? Relate Lalor to Karl Marx. Develop the concept of primitive communism as the basic original arrangement of land-tenure in this country.

Alice Milligan We may have to print your article with an editorial disclaimer.

Yeats Mr Milligan, come here. Who is this dangerous man
> Slouching, as it were, towards Bethlehem to be born?

Milligan I think we should all listen to him: I think it is his turn.
> Already things have been spoken I have never before heard said.

Exeunt.

SCENE 11

Enter GRABITALL *and* EMPLOYERS. *The latter are hanging up strings of bunting and erecting coloured lights and heraldic devices of the royal arms, etc. A big banner at the back with the message 'Victoria Regina: 1837–1897: Sixty Glorious Years!'*

Grabitall The British Empire roars and cheers
> World-wide for sixty glorious years.
> Australia – there it goes!*
> New Zealand* – Canada, the far-flung northern snows* –
> The African, the Indian, black as night,
> Bellow and yelp their loyal royal delight† –
> As drums and guns and gongs and singsong girls declare
> The joyful pandemonium of this great imperial year . . .!
> From Ireland too we want to hear a cheer.

Employers God Save the Queen!
> And let it be made known
> That loyalty, independence and Home Rule
> Can all together ring the Dublin bell!
> We here hang out our bunting, row on row
> From Dublin Castle to the Phoenix Park,
> Illuminate the lot when it gets dark,

> * Cheers (offstage)
> † Cheers and some booing (offstage)

> While up and down the mounted troopers go
> Deterring all intruders: this is a show
> We are determined to keep safe and sound:
> No sacrilege today on loyal Irish ground . . .

Grabitall Let there be light!

The illuminations begin to go on: amidst gasps and cheers from the crowds who have drifted in. CONNOLLY *appears at one corner and addresses the audience:*

Connolly A certain member, who shall be nameless, of the ISRP, being employed all unsuspected by the Dublin Electricity Company, has his hand upon the switch that has just made this crucial connection. To him alone the responsibility of turning nightfall into a simulacrum of the aurora borealis: to him alone the responsibility for what happens next!

More and more lights go on: and the cheers are redoubled. Suddenly: complete darkness.

Ha ha, me bould Barney: you're dead on the minute!

Lantern slides appear on a wall surface as the crowd groans with disappointment. They illustrate statistics and scenes of famine and emigration. The crowd, astonished, giggles, laughs, and in places gives yells of outrage.

Implacable as Queen Jezebel in an upper window of Rutland Square Miss Maud Gonne applies her timeless beauty to the ephemera of modern science. Sure 'tis no more than a smokey old magic lantern –

> But not the finger of God on the wall of Belshazzar the proud
> Wrote for his doom and foreboding one word so much to be
>   feared.

The illuminations come on again.

Ah: well, we didn't think Barney could keep his hand on the switch for ever. But don't go away now – we're not finished by a long way.

Vulgar music playing a funeral march is heard – kazoos, etc. A group of demonstrators enter slowly, carrying a coffin with a black pall reading 'The Corpse of the British Empire'. Yeats is in the lead, and they sing:

Coffin-bearers
> Here comes the empire, carry it away
> Throw it in the river, tip it to the sea:
> For it is dead and rotten it is dead and rotten –
> Here comes the empire carry it away . . .

POLICE *rush in to intercept.*

Grabitall Break every head: they shall not cross the bridge!

Connolly (*puts himself beside* YEATS) Get it to the river – tip it over the edge!

After a scuffle the coffin is got to the edge of the stage and thrown over.

Here goes the coffin of the British Empire!
To hell with the British Empire –
Into the Liffey and out into the sea – !

The POLICE, *outmanoeuvred, now attack the demonstration with savagery.
At the end of the fray, they are left holding* CONNOLLY.

After all that, it was not surprising they put the handcuffs upon
me.
And yet, the following morning, after one cold night in gaol,
When I came up before the magistrate, he did not want to look a
fool.

Enter MAGISTRATE: CONNOLLY *is placed before him.* MAUD GONNE *and*
YEATS *re-enter.*

They could not prove I had incited anyone to rape, burn, or kill –
The more fuss they made about it, the more it would be talked of
abroad,
And in India, Ceylon, Africa, men and women who had roared
God Save the Queen as loud as any would maybe wonder had
they done wrong:
Seeing their views were not shared by the greatest poet in the
English tongue . . .

Maud Gonne Mr Yeats was not arrested, being a member of the middle classes.

Yeats Nonetheless it was well-known that from behind these gleaming glasses
The inspiration for the demonstration had originally shot out like
fire.

Magistrate
I shall fine you one pound and I also require
You give recognisances for good behaviour or whatever else needs
to be said . . .

Maud Gonne
Whatever else means this much: an old woman today lies dead
Because the metropolitan police of Dublin cracked open the skull
of her head
When all she was trying to do was get away home out of the
crowd.

Magistrate Clear the court!

Prompted by MAUD GONNE, YEATS *pays money to a* POLICEMAN *and gets a
receipt.*

Connolly I remain here to make the statement that I do not intend to pay this
fine –

Policeman It's paid, we have the money, there's the receipt.
Maud Gonne (*to* CONNOLLY) Don't argue – go home – come along . . .
He looks inclined to dispute it: but everyone else goes away and he is left alone, with MAUD GONNE, *who leads him away.*

SCENE 12

Noise of a child crying all through the scene.

Connolly Lillie – where are you, Lillie? Safe and sound, my love – we are here – !

Enter LILLIE, *with a baby wrapped up in her shawl, very worried.*

Lillie Your daughter Nora has been sick all day:
    I asked the doctor what was wrong
    And all he said to me was that he could not say.
    I asked him did he think there could be any danger:
    He told me he could not tell, that in the end I would discover
    That all sickness in these streets is as dangerous as yellow fever.
    He gave me some medicine that would do nothing but keep her
        quiet –
    Which it does not as you can hear, she makes more noise than
        your last night's political riot –
    And *I* am left to do nothing but sit by her bed and wait.
    And holding *this* one: how about that . . .?

She is angrily trying to do housework and nurse the baby at the same time. GRABITALL *enters at one side.*

Connolly My God will she do nothing but thrust up her backbone and greet – ?
    Here, Lillie, let me take her –
Lillie In God's name, which is worse:
    A rake of a husband rolling all hours in and out of the public
        house
    Or this wilful political libertine who prefers his own pride and a
        Bridewell cell?
Grabitall Secure in the knowledge that his fine will be paid
    By an elegant educated unmarried lady – oh she never scrubbed a
        floor in her life:
    From the breeding and burden of children such loveliness we
        suppose is kept safe . . .?
Maud Gonne
    He bites his lip, is well aware,
    He does not dare
    To speak one word.

Lillie You need not tell me you believe
   That man has not been born to lead
   Nor woman from his lazy rib-bone built up only to serve.
   You need not tell me when we are so poor
   That by my strength behind this tenement door
   Yourself are strengthened all the more
   To stand out in the street and state
   That you at least alone will not accept defeat.
   If I stand out with you our children could not eat.
   All last night I filled my empty arms with hate.
   I now declare it.
   James, what I have said, you need not say again.

Connolly You know and I know we must do what we have always done.
   But I was not in the street alone:
   Not only Mr Yeats and Miss Maud Gonne –
   You also I saw walking when we threw that coffin down.

Maud Gonne
   I saw Eire the goddess walking and she wore a robe of green.

Connolly And *I* saw a large element of a large class of the ragged riffraff of
   Dublin,
   Their potato-faces split with a very dirty grin . . .
   There is no recrimination over what is best to be done.

Maud Gonne
   No recrimination, and no *doubt*, surely, over what is to be done:
   We must immediately get ready to raise the ghost of bold Wolfe
    Tone!
   The centenary is very near
   We have no more than a year
   We may be sure that if last night there were heads broken in
   Next year they will crack all bones between kneecap and chin:
   Mon Dieu but we have them rattled,
   The great wolf-hounds have picked up the scent . . .

Lillie Miss Gonne, I mean Madame Gonne, came round here, James, while
you were in prison this morning.

   She paid for the doctor
   She paid for the rent
   She did almost everything for me it was possible to resent:
   And now both of us are so grateful
   She was so offhand and so cool –
   Had either of us said anything
   We would have felt such a churl and a fool.

 Exeunt.

END OF ACT 1

ACT 2: 'Alarums and Excursions'

SCENE 1

A bird's-eye view of Dublin around its bay, with the Georgian buildings rearing up amongst the slums. The whole guarded by redcoat soldiers and police. (Back-cloth 3.)

Enter GRABITALL *and a* CIVIL SERVANT.

Grabitall How does it happen that the man Connolly was fined no more than one pound? Confound it, sir: he completely disrupted the Queen's jubilee!

Civil Servant Yes indeed, one pound . . . Not altogether so small a sum as it sounds. I understand he's out of work.

Grabitall He did not have to pay it himself. His impudence has not been quenched, rather is it aggravated. To commemorate the insurrection of seventeen ninety-eight is potentially a most serious challenge to the entire concept of the political union between Ireland and Britain. I am well aware these street demonstrations are the work of no more than a trivial minority – but we must understand that they not only occur – they are *seen* to occur by a significant body of persons – within a very short time they will become the accepted thing. There is only one thing to be accepted in Ireland at this time: and that is the continued benefit to all of her people of the Imperial system. I will only believe that that is believed when the Dublin mob itself puts paid to this man Connolly and these renegade gentlefolk who encourage him to his nonsense. The jubilee crowds were distinctly heard by the police to be cheering and laughing and egging him on.

Civil Servant Do you suppose if Her Majesty herself had been in Dublin –

Grabitall Are you mad? Would you have her insulted to her face?

Civil Servant I don't think she would have been. The face was far distant, the concept is abstract – so nobody cared. But if Her Majesty were to show that she cares for Dublin – I mean a personal relationship, a direct communication – she is a very gracious lady –

Grabitall Out of the question! Of course . . . we could get hold of a Duke . . . The Duke of York!

Civil Servant Sir, the very man! Happily married, entirely non-political. The Duchess as well. They say she is most popular.

Grabitall Doesn't matter what she's *said* to be – we have to prove that she *is*. Leave nothing to chance. Assemble a suitable crowd for the occasion – people in government service would be best –

Civil Servant And their wives –

Grabitall Soldiers off duty –
Civil Servant Policemen –
Grabitall Castle officials –
Civil Servant Military pensioners –
Grabitall And their wives!

> *A crowd assembles, with the* EMPLOYERS, *who distribute small union jacks to wave.*

Are we ready?

> *A* POLICE OFFICER *button-holes the* CIVIL SERVANT *and whispers in his ear.*

Civil Servant Just one moment . . . Good God, we can't have that!
Grabitall What's the matter?
Civil Servant: The Irish Socialist Republican Party has announced a special meeting of the most radical of the seventeen ninety-eight commemoration committees to coincide with the arrival of the Duke and Duchess.
Grabitall We can't have that!
Civil Servant I have said so. The police are taking action. Wait a moment –

> POLICE *start moving across the stage. The* CIVIL SERVANT *intercepts them:*

– now be very very careful!
Grabitall (*snatches a drawn sabre from a* POLICE OFFICER) Action – what sort of action? Good God, we can't have *this*! Get me the superintendant!
Civil Servant No no, sir, it's too late – the Duke of York is already here!
Grabitall Cross your fingers, touch wood, say a prayer, we've got to go through with it! Bring on the Duke of York!

> *To the tune of 'The Grand Old Duke of York' puppets representing the* DUKE *and* DUCHESS *are trundled across the stage. The crowds wave and cheer. From the middle of the crowd* CONNOLLY *bursts forward with a green banner unfurled which reads 'Truth Freedom and Justice in Ireland'. The* DUKE *and* DUCHESS *are hustled away in panic, the* POLICE *set upon the crowd, trying to reach* CONNOLLY, *but hitting all sorts of people in the process.* CONNOLLY *escapes, and the stage is cleared of all save* GRABITALL *and the* CIVIL SERVANT.

SCENE 2

Civil Servant Do you want to see the newspapers?
Grabitall I do not.
Civil Servant The Germans in particular were extremely amused.
Grabitall There were no arrests. Why not?
Civil Servant I don't think the police were able to catch anyone . . .
Grabitall Twice . . . in two months! And you were the clever fellow who told

me it might be possible to 'pre-determine' the tone of the commemoration of Tone . . . I was not making jokes for you to laugh at, you fool. Wolfe Tone was a republican; had his rebellion been successful, he would have set up in Ireland a secular, egalitarian, revolutionary state which would have joined with Napoleon in the total destruction of the kingdom of Great Britain – my God, in the scales of history that man would have outweighed Nelson – Trafalgar would have been reversed, Waterloo could never have happened. You and I would be on one level: and a rude labourer like James Connolly would hold the power of life and death over both of our heads!

Civil Servant But Wolfe Tone was not successful – he died a martyr, he is revered by both labourer and industrialist –

Grabitall Catholic and protestant –

Civil Servant Creditor and debtor . . . He is all things to all men. And therein lies his danger. Any one group among all those groups can take him over and exploit him.

Grabitall It is up to us to ensure that *we* determine *which* group.

> The old old tale
> Divide-and-rule
> If the workers push
> Then the bosses must pull . . .

We'll start with religion. Wolfe Tone was a protestant, therefore in the north the sacred memory of the damned cut-throat must be made the exclusive property of the most bigoted catholic faction! Call down to me Wee Joe Devlin!

Civil Servant Mr Devlin, we want a word!

Calls for 'Mr Devlin!' receding offstage. After a pause, enter DEVLIN.

Devlin I heard ye say cut-throat . . .
> It's a lie and a damned lie.
> Never never never could a brave Irish lad
> By his own hand come to die.
> For if he did he would go to hell.
> He was murdered, in his cell.
> He shot straight into the arms of God –
> How can we describe such a one as a dirty prod?

Civil Servant
> Can you make it clear to all Belfast town
> That gallant young Tone
> Was one of your own?

Devlin You give me the word – it shall be done!
> With priest and bishop and bell and book
> We hang him up high on our Roman hook!

As he goes out an ORANGEMAN *enters with a drum.*

Orangeman Do we hear Wee Joe Devlin hail the name of Wolfe Tone?
        Then we drown him with the drumming of the Battle of the
        Boyne!

He goes out after DEVLIN, *making a dreadful noise on his drum. Enter* ALICE
MILLIGAN.

Alice Milligan That clear enough marks the end of any republican commemoration in the north. Where on earth is Maud Gonne? If she doesn't
take care, an equivalent dirty trick is about to be played in Dublin.
Grabitall In Dublin mad Maude Gonne
        And James Connolly all on their own
        Have prepared a celebration
        Directly linked to revolution.
        If Crookey and O'Hookey can be got on their committee
        They will split, they will split
        And the world will weep for pity . . .

Enter EMPLOYERS.

        Who is the man to get them there?

Enter YEATS, *dreamily.*

Civil Servant (*looks at him*)
        Mr William Butler Yeats, with his long poetic hair . . .
        (*To* YEATS) Mr Yeats, you are a protestant – don't you think it would be
desirable, in the interests of the education of the soul of the whole
nation, if these well-meaning but perhaps fumbling decent catholic men
from shop and counting-house –
1st Employer We're more than that, we're more than that –
3rd Employer
        In the parliament of Westminster
        We each one of us hold a seat!
Civil Servant Just so . . . don't you think, Mr Yeats, it is your duty as a leading
cultural figure to reject nobody from the arrangements of this patriotic
epiphany?
Yeats The word *epiphany* is very nice.
        I am happy to lend my best efforts to splice
        In the rope of national unity every frayed and broken strand.
        Mr Crookey, Mr O'Hookey, I rejoice to shake your hand . . .

GRABITALL *and the* CIVIL SERVANT *withdraw discreetly.* ALICE MILLIGAN
goes out, shaking her head ominously. The EMPLOYERS *examine the decorations which are still hanging where they were put up for the Jubilee.*

3rd Employer A question of economy on the public manifestations – we can

make a job of it here with this yoke and keep all th'expenses down –
YEATS *starts removing imperial symbols from the decorations.* 3RD EM-
PLOYER *stops him: and takes from him a large shield of the royal arms.*
Merciful hour: ye'd think these bloody poets had never handled a petty
cash return in their lives at all at all . . .

He reverses the royal arms and reveals the Irish Harp on the back.

Don't ye see, two in one – sure, th'underside of th'skirts of tyranny
reveals th'intimate garments of th'goddess of God-given Liberty!

*They turn all the shields round in this way. The biggest one, in the middle,
proves to have the royal arms on both sides.* 1ST EMPLOYER *studies it in
perplexity.*

No no no – turn it round, man, turn it round, have some sense of chro-
matic relevance!
1st Employer Sure, amn't I after turning it?
3rd Employer I think we have a tentative problem here . . . so what'd we do?
1st Employer So what's to prevent us from modifying it, so?

He drapes a band of green ribbon transversely across the shield. MAUD
GONNE *enters and watches what is happening.*

Maud Gonne Willie, in the Name of God, what do you think you are doing!
Yeats (*up a ladder with his mouth full of tacks*) Hallo there! I'm only –
Maud Gonne (*points to the 'modified' shield*) Good heavens, that's out for a
start! Will you please take it down.
3rd Employer
    Excuse me, Miss Maud Gonne –
    The good work which you began,
    By our own efforts and contribution
    Is now brought to its fruition.

1ST EMPLOYER *brings in a large medallion of the Wolfe Tone profile, which
is hung underneath the 'modified' royal arms. Music begins: 'The Wearing
of the Green'. A crowd assembles with green flags.* GRABITALL *and the*
CIVIL SERVANT *join the* EMPLOYERS *in a formal group in front of the medallion.* CONNOLLY *enters near Maud Gonne.*

    Mr Devlin out of Ulster
    Has come to help our function prosper.

Enter DEVLIN *with a* PRIEST *and they join the central group.*

Devlin Mr Devlin from Belfast
    Has brought with him a holy priest.
Priest (*deferred to by all, takes pride of place*) Wolfe Tone, we must remember,
was a man of his own time, and much of what he said and did has of
course been rendered redundant by the progressive spiritual enlighten-

ment of the modern age. Had God made it possible for him to have
received his education at the catholic college of Maynooth – he surely
would never have – –

Connolly Enough, enough!
 This dreadful stuff
 Can never be endured!
 Miss Gonne, my party will have no part
 Of *this*!
 Are we assured
 As we walk out
 That you as well walk out with us?

He stalks out with some ISRP members who have joined him.

Maud Gonne
 I do not know, I cannot say
 It breaks my heart to play no part
 Upon this great centenary day.
 Willie, what have you done?
Yeats My love, my heart, my dear Miss Gonne,
 I did it for the best . . .
Maud Gonne
 All finished, disintegrated –
 What will they think of us in the west . . . ?

The PRIEST *has now completed his eulogy.* GRABITALL *comes over to* MAUD
GONNE.

Grabitall Because the clergy participated
 They will think it both meet and fit.
 So do I. I take off my hat.
 Dulce et decorum est pro patria mori . . .
Priest My friends, this pregnant sacramental story –
1st Employer This supreme sacrifice –
3rd Employer Of sugar and spice –
Devlin And all things nice –
Priest *Requiescat in pace* for the honour and glory –
1st Employer Of national Irish biscuits and bread –
3rd Employer
 Patriotically packed in boxes of wood –
 There's a little leaflet handed round we'd be glad to have read –

The EMPLOYERS *distribute advertising literature to the crowd:*

1st Employer Advertising our products with decency and taste –
Devlin Appropriate to the solemnity of the present occasion –
Grabitall And thank God we've got rid of all thought of revolution!

Everybody claps politely. CONNOLLY *suddenly appears through the crowd selling newspapers.*

Connolly (*very raucous*) *The Workers' Republic* – buy *The Workers' Republic*! Buy the first socialist newspaper to be published in Ireland! Buy the *only* socialist newspaper to be published in Ireland! Buy *The Workers' Republic*! Read *The Workers' Republic*!

> Ha ha ye did not think we'd have this ready quite so sharp!
> Aye there's more than one string to the old minstrel's broken
>   harp . . .

GRABITALL *and all the Wolfe Tone celebrants leave rapidly.* MAUD GONNE *remains.*

Maud Gonne
> Well enough: but I am afraid it will do little good.
> I see no course but to revert to the old oath-bound Brotherhood.

Connolly Conspiracy? Secret terror?
> You walk blindfold in a bog of error.
> Liberty and justice should not need
> Like criminals to hide their head.
> Cry socialism aloud in the open field
> And let its logic be revealed
> To all for all for ever . . .

Buy *The Workers' Republic*, read *The Workers' Republic*!

> And yet I must admit it true
> That had this Brotherhood not worked concealed
> Known only to a few
> Year after year
> The weight of slavery in our long dark night
> Would have crushed us utterly with despair.

Maud Gonne I wish I could believe that you were right . . .

Exit MAUD GONNE.

SCENE 3

Connolly Buy *The Workers' Republic*, read *The Workers' Republic* –

He sings:

> Every Friday once a week
> Keen in the claw and long in the beak

Fierce as an eagle overhead
It costs ye a penny, it's worth a whole quid!

They said that we were very small
They could not hear us, not at all,
They mocked us and they'd shout us down,
They watched us sink and they hoped we'd drown.

Sure it beats in my hand, the sap in the wood,
The root in the ground and the pea in the pod,
The egg in the hen, the salt in the soup.
You start from nothing, it's your only hope . . .!

He passes up and down among the audience, offering them the papers and making as though people have put questions to him.

A few simple answers to a few simple questions. Congratulations, Jim, we never thought you'd get it out, and where in the name of God did the money come from? In the heel of the hunt from yourselves, subscriptions, collections, beg, borrow, scrape it and save – and fifty pounds in a lump sum from Keir Hardie over in Britain. Who prints it? A small man in a back street. And he doesn't overcharge. But have we got enough money to carry on paying the bills? The answer to that one is definite: no. Unless more people buy it next week than are buying it this week and more the week after that than are buying it next week. What's in it? So let me tell you: eight pages; with a poem by my old friend John Leslie, very appropriately upon Wolfe Tone; an attack upon sectarianism; a few articles by yours truly upon the origins of modern war, which I attribute to the struggle of the capitalists for more markets for their produce; the inevitable instability of land-ownership in rural Ireland leading to the present disastrous famine in the west; a demand for political action by trade unionists: and a vigorous opinion upon the revival of the Gaelic language.

Enter ALICE MILLIGAN.

Alice Milligan Which is what?
Connolly That in general and isolation it's an admirable idea: but also it is quite impractical to teach a starving man *any* language.

She shakes her head ominously.

Enter MILLIGAN. *He is followed by* O'BRIEN *and other ISRP members.*

Milligan I have already heard that in Belfast
By the very title of your paper an entire market has been lost.
Connolly How's that?

Milligan Socialism in the north can never be republican.

Connolly Republicanism in the south can never be socialist. I've heard both notions *ad nauseam*. I don't believe either. I have set forward my arguments: and I'm happy to inform you that my point of view is supported from an unexpected area of the highest authority. I have here a letter from Mrs Eleanor Aveling, in London. Her husband has decided to take up associate membership of the ISRP for which purpose she encloses a postal order for one shilling. Now that's not a laugh. It's good news of enormous potential consequence.

O'Brien Mrs Eleanor Aveling?

Milligan Who the deuce is Mrs Aveling?

Connolly Ha ha she is none other than the daughter of Karl Marx!
According to her father's word, the English working class
Will never accomplish anything until it has first got rid
Of the problem of Ireland. Now surely, surely what he said
Is proof enough for the thickest head
In Ulster that national independence must come first!

Milligan There's more to it than that. An Ulster catholic bishop has condemned the new newspaper.

O'Brien Isn't that what we want? So the protestants after all will buy the unfortunate rag?

Connolly Will they not? Not? Then why not?

Milligan Don't you see that they will see it as a particularly subtle jesuitical trick by the bishop designed to promote the paper by stealth?
Mr Connolly, it's very clear
That the full ramifications of the Ulster complication
Are so remote from you down here
That you cannot yet have the remotest conception
Of our Belfast capacity for self-mutilation.

Connolly H'm . . . but on the other hand with such a newspaper we must expect and welcome controversy. It cannot be a bad thing that on both sides of the religious-political divide –

Alice Milligan Mr Connolly, in Ulster, the controversy has not even begun to take place! The paper has not been purchased!

Connolly How many Irishmen live in America? I have here a letter from Daniel De Leon, chairman of the Socialist Labor Party of the United States.

Milligan He can't be an Irishman.

Connolly He's a Jew. And in his party there are Italians, and Irish, and Germans, and Greeks; protestant, catholic, orthodox, hebrew – who cares? They're all socialists: and they have *heard* of us, d'you see! De Leon has a weekly newspaper – he asks me for a series of articles on the famine in the west – Maud Gonne has gone to Mayo – I go out there to join her and I write upon what I see. De Leon also tells me that he has made use of our manifesto to get Irish-Americans to vote for the socialists in the municipal elections. We must send him a letter of solidarity – can you draft one?

MILLIGAN *makes a note.*

And do what you can for God's sake in Belfast – if the working class won't read it, at least get the damn thing circulated among your literary intelligentsia – I daresay in those quarters you're not intimidated by the bishop or disturbed in your dreams at night by mad Fenians with bloody pitchforks . . .?

Exeunt MILLIGANS

O'Brien We have municipal elections of our own for the first time next year.

Connolly With the benevolent Tory intention of keeping us quiet in our own wallow. Well, we must take advantage – put up at least one candidate – bark, howl, break our teeth upon the bars –

Tom Lyng I don't know that we can afford it.

Connolly It's sheer waste to put out political print without a living man at the election to embody what we call for. Very well: we need a candidate. The North Dock ward of Dublin, the paper has sold well there – particularly because of our articles attacking the liquor-trade. Comrade Stewart?

Stewart Now I did warn you if you asked me I could guarantee you no success . . . But I daresay on the relevant subjects such as schools, unemployment relief, hospital services and cetera, I can throw together something to make some of 'em sit up. I have taken pains to make a comprehensive study.

Connolly I've advised Stewart his main platform should be a straightforward statement of the incontrovertible fact that the public welfare of Dublin is a European disgrace . . . Any questions?

O'Brien I have. There's a whole bagful of candidates calling themselves Labour being put up not only in Dublin but in all corners of the country. Our attitude towards 'em?

Connolly Watchful in the extreme. Any candidate that says Labour, let him prove it by his policy. If he's able to do so, the columns of *The Workers' Republic* are thrown open to him free of charge. The paper will make the candidate, the candidate will make the paper: with the newspaper and the candidate and the electorate all together we will construct the political party – and then . . .!

They all disperse, except CONNOLLY.

SCENE 4

Connolly And then indeed – then, what? Success . . .?

Such was the confidence I did profess
In this, the mighty engine of the press.
Pride, pride – however hard we tried, we could not sell
Sufficient newspapers to pay the printers' bill.
No bourgeois newspaper, no public hall
Was open to our revolutionary call:
Just as in Edinburgh, the parties of the rich and fat
Took care of that.
The spokesman for the lean and poor
Knocked every day upon an iron-barred door.
Sackcloth and ash! We took a bash:
And in the end we ran clean out of cash . . .

The PARTY MEMBERS *straggle in again, dejected.*

Is there nobody in this farcical organisation that knows how to keep an account? Look at this for Godsake, d'you call this an expenses-return!
Tom Lyng Now there's no call to be blackguarding us – them expenses was called for in a hell of a hurry to get the candidate home from a particularly rough meeting – with the priests that was in it driving the mob on to us with sticks from the porch of the pro-Cathedral – do you expect me to ask the cab-driver to take the time to give a receipt?
Connolly Aye . . . This torn-up cigarette-packet, when we examine it properly, is the root of the entire problem. Dressed, as it were, in an envelope of obscure rags, we conceal in every fold and turn-up a penny here – a ha'penny here – and God preserve us, here's a shilling!

He is making a pantomime of searching his clothes. The coins are real.

Who'd ha' thought it – in the hem of a waistcoat-lining! No, it's not: it's a tin-plate button! Indeed, we have the mentality of a street mendicant, a professional at that. And we're a bob down on the final score unless we can find one in our sock. It won't do.
O'Brien It's just ridiculous.
Connolly So what did I tell you?
Jack Lyng So what next?
Connolly Under no circumstances whatever can we abandon the notion of a newspaper.
Tom Lyng All right. Once we've had it, we can't do without it.
Stewart If I'd have had the cash that's been sunk into that newspaper, I could have hired halls all over Dublin for the conduct of me meetings.
Connolly You know perfectly well it was not the *cost* of the halls that stopped it –
O'Brien Overt political censorship by the committees that controlled them.
Stewart I'm not persuaded of that.
Connolly Well I am. So let's have less of it, putting the whole blame on the

bloody paper. For which at this present moment, we are not able to afford a printer. So we print it ourselves.

O'Brien Us? Who?

Connolly If necessary, me. At eleven years old I was handling type in a printing-office.

Stewart Sure, this'll all take ages. To get even one edition printed – let alone every week –

Jack Lyng And we're still not going to be able to distribute in Belfast . . .

Connolly A weekly paper is impossible. Already the damn thing got to be so *weakly* that it lay down and died – what we will have to settle for is one that will appear whenever it becomes strong enough to put itself out . . . Joke . . . All right, lads, find some money. Find a press. Type. Ink. Paper. Why don't we find it today?

They all go off, busily. O'BRIEN *and* CONNOLLY *remain behind.*

SCENE 5

Connolly William, you're the treasurer. Now that's it . . .

He hands O'Brien all the money he has found in his suit.

That's my contribution.

O'Brien But this is –

Connolly Everything. Empty pockets. What am I to do? Oh, I get paid well enough for organising the party – seven shillings every week . . .

O'Brien When it ought to be twenty.

Connolly Aye, it *was* – for a while . . . I've tried all different classes of work – when I could get them. The heavy work destroys me – I mean, literally: I can't think. And for anything else the hours are all wrong, I'd have to give up the politics completely. William, what I really need to be is an independent capitalist. Your brother . . .

O'Brien He does have a little money, yes.

Connolly Look – if he could – just this once, mind – stake me out, say a matter of no more than two quid – I can get hold of a pedlar's pack and a stock of bits of nonsense – holy pictures, needles and thread – you know the kind of thing that old wives buy at the back door . . .?

O'Brien Together with a pair of trousers that don't exhibit what's normally hid . . .

Connolly What – ! Where – ?

Twisting himself round, he discovers a large hole worn in the seat of his pants.

Oh my God, no! It was not like that this morning!

O'Brien It is now. You turn up at a back door, so: you'll be in the Bridewell in five minutes. At all events, here's two quid. I'll get it back from the brother. And – moreover –

Like a conjurer, from the inside of his overcoat or somewhere he produces a new pair of trousers.

Connolly And where the deuce did you get those?

O'Brien There's a feller in my own trade – a little tailor's apprentice who works next door to the party-office – he sees you climbing the stairs every morning from below. The state of your backside has created him professional pain. Put them on.

Connolly But I can't afford –

O'Brien It's a gift. Put them on.

CONNOLLY *does so.*

Connolly It lowers me sufficiently in my own opinion, this whole business – I would be glad of an explanation of what you find in it so damned funny?

O'Brien Jasus, he's read your pamphlets but he's never really looked at *you*. I'm afraid he's gone and made them for a man with *straight* legs.

They both laugh.

Connolly Thank you. Thank you, William. William, you're a good man . . .

O'BRIEN *goes and fetches a pedlar's pack and a tray for* CONNOLLY *and then goes out.*

Connolly (*sings*)
<blockquote>
With a song upon my lips
And a pack upon my back
I wander through the wilderness
Upon my weary track.

O do you want a button-hook
Or do you want a stay
Or a pair of laces for your boots . . .?
And if you want them, can you pay?

For all is rock and stone
And barren all around:
I once was told a story
There was gold beneath the ground.

It won't be found by digging
Nor by searching on a chart:
But maybe when you're three parts dead
You'll fall and burst your heart.
</blockquote>

> Then if you could but see it,
> The place wherein you are
> The rocky reef you lie upon
> Would glitter like a star . . .!

Exit.

SCENE 6

A landscape devastated by war – broken trees and buildings, wrecked vehicles, dead men and horses, etc. (Backcloth 4.)

Enter 1ST *and* 3RD EMPLOYERS *in safari gear (English colonial accents). They are in the last stages of exhaustion and collapse on the ground. They have an* AFRICAN BEARER *with them, loaded down with baggage.*

3rd Employer (*after a pause, scrabbles in front of him*) My God – ! Crook, look here – ! My God, Crook, we've found gold! We are rich – rich – rich – !

1st Employer Too late . . . no good . . . water . . . Hook, we must have water!

Bearer (*stands like a statue*) Bwana – I smell water.

Enter a BOER.

Boer (*aggressively to* 3RD EMPLOYER) Man, do you dare set your profane feet upon the sanctified pastures of the people of God?

(*To the* BEARER)

You, you damn Kaffir – stand away when a white man's talking or I'll take the hide off your black back!

He beats the BEARER, *who does not offer resistance or flinch, but moves slowly back a couple of steps. The* BOER *holds out a water bottle to the* EMPLOYERS.

Now – you – I give you water that you may not perish in your affliction: you have drunken it: you will depart. The husbandry of these fields is for the people of God alone and no outlander of the unregenerate shall enter it unto them nor covet them, upon pain of mortal chastisement. Go!

3rd Employer Just one moment, sir, if you please . . .

He is scooping something up from the ground into his helmet.

Boer Ha! You find gold. You find death. It has been written: in the scriptures. Therefore, we do not dig. We shall not prevent *you* – if indeed you are an-hungered for your own self-destruction. But of course you will pay. And of course in our congregation you will not lift up your voice. So there you are. Dig.

He stands back, and they dig furiously, shovelling up and piling gold. The BOER *then siezes a large amount of it.*

My percentage. I assess this according to the laws and commandments of the people of God.
1st Employer Mr Hook?
3rd Employer Mr Crook?
1st Employer I say, Hook, this is not right. Find a phrase.
3rd Employer 'No taxation without representation'?
1st Employer Yes: we demand democracy!
Boer Outlander and unregenerate – get off my land *now*! I said put down that spade!

Scuffle. The BOER *knocks* 3RD EMPLOYER *down and puts his foot on him.* 1ST EMPLOYER *fires wildly, misses; and in turn is wounded by a shot from the* BOER. *The scuffle develops into a regular battle. The fighting should be suggested symbolically by the hurling of rolls of toilet paper and the like. The* BOER *has the advantage. The* BEARER *remains on the stage throughout this episode – the combatants ignore him most of the time: but also use him as a shield, an aiming-rest, etc.* . . . .

1st Employer Help help. Help help. Discrimination. Help!

Enter GRABITALL.

Grabitall This gold was found for me to lift up my shares and stocks:
    No choice but to deliver these incompetent cowardly blocks –
    Their cry resounds upon the arid plain:
    It is not heard in vain.
    You greedy bigot – back! Before the army of the Queen
    With gun and drum and bugle turns
    Your God into a thornbush and your promised land
    Into a valley of dry bones . . .
Boer If I run out of bullets I will repel you with thrown stones.

The battle rages. MAUD GONNE *crosses the front of the stage.*

Maud Gonne (*en passant*)
    The Boer Republic sets its back
    Against the rock
    And stands the shock –
    It is not right
    Such noble independence all alone should fight
    Without assistance and support . . .

She goes. Enter GERMAN *and* FRENCH ARMS MERCHANTS *with loads of symbolic ammunition, which they load upon the* BOER, *glaring in rivalry meanwhile at each other.*

German Arms Merchant
> My friend, by way of lawful trade,
> My pleasure now to offer aid:
> From Germany from the firm of Krupp.
> *Gott in Himmel:* do not give up!

French Arms Merchant
> The power of death from *La Belle France*:
> Perfidious Albion must not advance!
> With cartridges and French cold steel
> Such capability to kill . . .!

Grabitall (*fetches ammunition for the* EMPLOYERS)
> For Vickers-Armstrong and Lee-Enfield I am an accredited agent –

He goes up to the other two MERCHANTS

> Gentlemen, don't you think we can come to some agreement:
> Let me whisper in your ear –
> We don't want anyone to hear . . .?

He gets into a huddle with the ARMS MERCHANTS *on the fringe of the renewed fighting.*

German Arms Merchant
> Dreadnoughts, howitzers, dirigible zeppelins, machine-guns,
> TNT –

Grabitall Submarines, torpedoes, dynamite, gelignite – of course for my usual fee –

French Arms Merchant
> Counting three hundred *mitrailleuses* for the value of one long-range gun.

Grabitall Subtracting from the cost of a first-rate ironclad cruiser –

French Arms Merchant
> Sixty per cent –

German Arms Merchant
> Seventy –

Grabitall Seventy-five?

All Three *Done . . .!*

They clasp hands on the bargain. The FRENCH *and* GERMAN ARMS MER-CHANTS *slip away.*

Grabitall My God the British army will too easily be beaten
> And the fighting brought to an end . . .!

3rd Employer
> You can find someone else to bloody well send!

German Arms Merchant (*as he goes out*)
> All this metal to manufacture . . .

French Arms Merchant (*on his way out*)
> And no use for it at all . . .?

Grabitall Bugler – sound the call!

The battlefield clears, the EMPLOYERS *and the* BOER *fighting each other off out of sight.* GRABITALL *takes hold of the* BEARER *and thrusts him out of the way of the characters entering for the next scene . . .*

A fanfare.

> You bloody dog, clear off, get out –
> We're dealing now with affairs of state!

SCENE 7

Enter PRIME MINISTER, TORY MP*s*, LIBERAL MP*s*, KEIR HARDIE.

Grabitall The Conservative government in parliament assembled, explains with some embarrassment the failure of its preliminary military campaign: and promises to do better.

Prime Minister We will do better.

Grabitall (*prompts him*) We will win!

Prime Minister Indeed we will win. Already we are introducing our formidable new weapon – the internment camp for civilians! But we demand an outright effort by the entire British Empire on behalf of the British Empire.

A pause.

> Well . . . Can we not hear from the Liberals, if you please . . . ?

1st Liberal Fervent response to the Prime Minister's fervent hope.

2nd Liberal Fervent denunciation of the fervent response.

1st Liberal Sit down.

2nd Liberal Shan't.

1st Liberal Traitor!

2nd Liberal Imperialist!

1st Liberal Why not? All the better for trade.

Grabitall Split. But as for Labour . . . ? No doubt firm to its fraternal idealism – Labour . . . ? Come, gentlemen, look sharp! The Prime Minister is waiting to pass the army estimates – enormously increased – Mr Keir Hardie, will you kindly make up your mind?

Keir Hardie The Independent Labour Party will not and cannot approve the forcible coercion of small and helpless nations.

A group of Labour supporters now thrust themselves forward.

Bernard Shaw Boers are backward!

Grabitall Mr George Bernard Shaw – of the Fabian Society.

The Webbs Even a Conservative government is more civilised than the Boers!

Grabitall Beatrice and Sydney Webb – of the Fabian Society.

Bernard Shaw If the Boers are not defeated they will oppress the black African –

The Webbs With mounting intensity, year after year, until our grandchildren and great grandchildren will be totally unable to do anything about it!

Bernard Shaw We ought to beat the Boers – here and now!

Keir Hardie Traitor.

Bernard Shaw Idiot.

The Webbs White supremacist.

Keir Hardie Paternalist.

Bernard Shaw Bigot!

Keir Hardie Imperialist!

Bernard Shaw Why not? All the better for the life-force of the human race.

Grabitall One war in the southern hemisphere
    And another war over here –
    The Conservatives alone see their object quite clear –

Exeunt all (save GRABITALL *and the* PRIME MINISTER) *scuffling and shouting mutual abuse.*

SCENE 8

Prime Minister
    While they thus wrangle up and down the hill
    The bugles call
    The ranks begin to fill –
Grabitall The unemployed prepare to kill.
    The fighting Irish manifest their well-known zeal
    For foreign blood; and flood
    Both north and south
    Into the gaping cannon-mouth . . .

Drums and bugles, etc. SOLDIERS *with colours pass and re-pass, marching with panache.*

    Crookey and O'Hookey know full well
    What drum to thump today, what tale to tell.

Enter 1ST *and* 3RD EMPLOYERS.

1st Employer (*sings*)
    The loyalty of Irishmen to the Queen of England's need –
3rd Employer (*sings*)
    Will prove to the Queen of England that the Irishmen indeed
    Are worthy of an independent parliament of their own:

1st Employer (*sings*)
>   And graciously she'll grant it them when once it has been shown
>   How be hundreds and be thousands they will fearlessly advance –

3rd Employer (*sings*)
>   To the forefront of the battle, boys, with never a backward
>   glance!

Employers (*sing*)
>   The war, the war, come forward to the war
>   And reap the reward of glory and gore . . .!

Prime Minister (*about to leave*) Thank you very much – good morning.

>   *Enter* CONNOLLY, MAUD GONNE, *and* O'BRIEN.

O'Brien Not so James Connolly. The Government
>   Assumes its rigorous attitude and declares –

Prime Minister
>   'THIS'.

O'Brien At once, with calm and dark intent
>   He claps upon his head his four-square hat,
>   Fixes his four-square features, and declares:

Connolly 'THAT'.

>   GRABITALL *and the* PRIME MINISTER *contemptuously go out.* CONNOLLY *and*
>   MAUD GONNE *take their places on a rostrum. People assemble to listen to*
>   *them.* O'BRIEN *unfurls a red banner reading 'ISRP opposes imperialist*
>   *war!'*

The meeting today of the Irish Socialist Republican Party is, as far as
I know, the first public protest to be held against the war anywhere in
the British Empire. This is a war that will undoubtedly take rank as
one of the most iniquitous wars of the century. Both the war itself, in
South Africa, and the condition of this country, are the work of a beast
of prey that is not to be moralised, converted, or conciliated. It can only
be destroyed!

Cheers.

England's difficulty should be Ireland's opportunity! For every soldier
required in Ireland to keep us from our true destiny is one less man to
prevent the Boers from determining their own future. Comrades, if we
can act upon our understanding of that fact, a very considerable portion
of the British army will not be sent to the Transvaal. Agitation for ourselves, and against the war, and against the Home Rule-Unionist twin
brethren who keep us apart in order to rob us, must begin, it must
continue, and it must increase every day until victory is achieved! Miss
Maud Gonne, whom you all know, has a resolution she wants to move.

O'Brien The resolution condemns –

Maud Gonne The criminal aggression of the British government.

O'Brien The resolution proposes –
Maud Gonne Meetings of protest to be held all over Ireland.
O'Brien The resolution urges –
Maud Gonne That every Irishman who has emigrated to South Africa should
    immediately take up arms against Her Majesty's Forces and in defence
    of the Boer Republic! The first man to do that – *par l'amour du bon Dieu* –
    I swear that I will marry him!

Enormous cheering.

O'Brien The resolution is unanimously passed. The resolution is overtly
    seditious – the police do not interfere.

The meeting breaks up. Exeunt all save GRABITALL. *As the stage clears*
O'BRIEN showers leaflets all over like confetti. GRIFFITH, *who has entered*
during the speeches with a green banner reading 'Sinn Fein opposes
British war in South Africa', throws his literature about, too.

SCENE 9

Enter a breathless POLICE OFFICER.

Grabitall And *why* did the police not interfere?
Police Officer Insufficient men on the ground at the time, sir.

GRABITALL *picks up one of* GRIFFITH's *papers – the* OFFICER *one of* O'BRIEN's.

Grabitall How the devil is he printing it?

O'BRIEN *re-passes across the stage calling* 'Read The Workers' Repub-
lic . . .'
O'Brien (*to audience, as he goes out again*)
    All on his own, as he said he would do it: he says it and he does it.
Grabitall Find it out then and suppress it.

The OFFICER *shrugs helplessly.*

    There's a printer's name at bottom of this sheet
    Emblazoned clear as paint: do you dare claim
    You do not know the premises whence it came?
Police Officer (*looks at the paper* GRABITALL *holds out to him*)
    You are too hot, sir. This is not the same.
    This is a paper published by Sinn Fein.
Grabitall I'm reading it!
    Not an infinitive that is not split.
    So typical. But listen! 'Irishmen:
    The freedom-loving patriotic Boer must win!
    If Saxon crudity in Africa prevail

Farewell farewell the liberty of the Gael!'
Why, this is twice as bad as is the other –
Suppress them now, suppress them both together!

Exit POLICE OFFICER. CONNOLLY *and* GRIFFITH *re-enter with their bundles
of newspapers.*

Connolly Come buy *The Workers' Republic*! Buy it today!
Tomorrow it may have vanished clean away!
Griffith Thus I defy the governmental ban –
Come buy, come buy *The United Irishman*!
Connolly (*looks sideways at* GRIFFITH)
Who pays to pave
The way for your brave paper – master or slave?
Grabitall So Connolly puts the question –
Arthur Griffiths thinks it comes from the wrong direction:
He was anticipating on his neck
A policeman's truncheon – answers with rebuke:
Griffith All of the Irish bend beneath subjection
And every man in Ireland without restriction
Has the right to pile such wealth as he is able.
What else is meant by freedom for the people?
I think, sir, we had better walk apart . . .
Connolly I think we had, my lad, with all my heart . . .

(*To audience*)

Good heavens, this is no time to be quarrelling with Arthur Griffith.
Just so we know where we stand – that's all.

Exit GRIFFITH.

SCENE 10

Enter O'BRIEN.

O'Brien Jim – Jim – Joseph Chamberlain –
Connolly Joseph Chamberlain – chief short-order-cook in Queen Victoria's
imperial chop-house – well?
O'Brien They've invited him to Trinity College, Dublin, to receive an
honorary degree. Now, Jim, this can be no coincidence!
Grabitall (*to audience*) Indeed it is not – we are losing the war: support for the
troops in the Transvaal must be drummed up – Joe Chamberlain in
Dublin will rally the loyalist cause!
Connolly (*formally, to audience*) The inevitable rally of protest that has been
organised receives nation-wide endorsement. Even Crookey and
O'Hookey are so alarmed they have consented to address it.

Crowds begin to come in again. O'BRIEN *unfurls a red banner reading 'No support for Imperialist Aggressors in Dublin'.* GRIFFITH *unfurls a green banner reading 'Reject British hypocrisy'.*

1ST *and* 3RD EMPLOYERS *enter.*

1st Employer Responsive as we are ever to the demands of our constituents –
3rd Employer And aware of the deleterious effect of the casualty-lists from South Africa on the ballot-box next time round, we have prepared a strong statement –
1st Employer Appealing to the British government –
3rd Employer To use its best endeavours –
1st Employer To patch up a peace with the Boers.
Grabitall Dissent must be destroyed – policemen, are you ready?

POLICE *assemble under his wing.*

Grabitall By order of the Lord Lieutenant, the rally of protest is forbidden!

The POLICE *deploy.*

The people are on the street, the police are on the street, the speakers –
3rd Employer (*slinks away from rostrum*) Have not arrived –
1st Employer Or if we did – we've all gone home . . .

Exeunt EMPLOYERS.

Grabitall So the crowd has no leadership, no focus, a herd of goats, break it up!
O'Brien James Connolly and Maud Gonne upon two wheels arrive:
⠀⠀⠀⠀The flag of the Boer Republic flying in the breeze –
⠀⠀⠀⠀An old experienced dust-collector knows how to drive,
⠀⠀⠀⠀Dodges with ease,

CONNOLLY *and* MAUD GONNE *move rapidly through the crowd as though he is driving a cart with her mounted behind him. She waves the Boer flag and holds a speech. The* POLICE *try to stop them but are hampered by the speed and movement of the crowd.*

⠀⠀⠀⠀The lady stands and sways and reads her –
Maud Gonne (*as she and* CONNOLLY *stop still for an instant*)
⠀⠀⠀⠀Treasonable speech!
O'Brien And then sits down –
⠀⠀⠀⠀James Connolly steers his reeling juggernaut
⠀⠀⠀⠀Three-quarters round the town –
⠀⠀⠀⠀Now he's arrested, now he's not –
⠀⠀⠀⠀The lady reads her –
Maud Gonne
⠀⠀⠀⠀Treasonable speech – again!
O'Brien To another crowd in another spot:
⠀⠀⠀⠀And then they all go home.

CONNOLLY, MAUD GONNE *and* O'BRIEN *go out. Everyone else disperses except* GRABITALL *and* POLICE, *who are left completely baffled – their helmets, knocked off in the scuffling, are strewn all over the stage.*

Grabitall I do not regard this evening's work as much of a success.

SCENE 11

Enter POLICE OFFICER.

Police Officer
> But sir, but sir, we've found his printing-press!
> What shall we do with it?

Two CONSTABLES *stagger in with a press*

Grabitall Batter it into scrap!

The POLICE *destroy the press.*

Police Officer
> The other chap?
Grabitall Griffith?
Police Officer
> I think, sir, when he hears of the rival journal's fate,
> His style of article will moderate –
> I think, sir, with a liberal wink, we could let pass
> The theoretical offerings of the middle class . . .?
Grabitall Sinn Fein: 'Ourselves Alone' . . .? Leave them alone.
Police Officer
> And yet, sir, I have heard it said
> That the old occult Republican Brotherhood
> Collects the cash for and has members in
> Your shapeless something of a vague Sinn Fein . . .
> 'Twould be grave implications were them two linked?
Grabitall Defunct – extinct –
> I am assured the Brotherhood is no more:
> It fell to pieces in the Land League War.
> It does not bear
> Upon the one political hard fact
> That recruiting for the army has hit rock-bottom
> With all this riot and vulgar ruction –
> There is the trend we have to counteract.

For a very sufficient reason. I have overdone it yet again. I have ground, according to my nature, the faces of the English poor so hard, and exploited them so mercilessly, that the military medical officers reject them as unfit. But Paddy – now – our rural Paddy, with his bacon and his cabbage and his buttermilk and strong potatoes – there is the material for interminable war – and I swear that I will have him! For if I don't – by God, I'm finished . . .! Political, electoral – have we done it – what's the news?

Enter 1ST *and* 3RD EMPLOYERS.

3rd Employer I am glad to report, sorr, that the moderate party of Home Rule in its various shapes and disguises has won the greater part of the votes upon all the local councils it contested. As for Labour –

1st Employer Devil a bit, sorr – banjaxed altogether – in the heel of the hunt not a socialist revolutionist got a seat in the entire country!

Enter CONNOLLY.

Connolly Brief statement from James Connolly explaining his defeat . . . I warned you last year and I warn you again this: that a Labour candidate who is no socialist is no good to the working classes. I am, however, more concerned – I would go so far as to say embittered – by the treatment we have received from the labour movement in Great Britain. I did not believe that they too would have cast us out: but from the throat of Keir Hardie we have heard the hue-and-cry . . .

Enter KEIR HARDIE – *he stands some way from* CONNOLLY *and they both speak to the audience.*

Keir Hardie I am exceedingly disappointed with the ISRP. There has been, of course, much sound and fury – Comrade Connolly for example at the head of a mob, brandishing a Boer flag and shouting, not only for an Irish Republic, but for the defeat of the British army! Why, what *is* the British army, what else but working men? In Britain, we have been struggling, year after year, for the formation of a strong and effective Parliamentary Labour Party . . . I was under the impression Comrade Connolly shared that struggle.

Connolly Who said I did not?

Keir Hardie By withdrawing as it were the socialists of catholic Ireland –

Connolly We are totally non-sectarian –

Keir Hardie That's what you call yourselves. But how many protestant workers in the north subscribe to your newspaper? By withdrawing as it were the socialists of catholic Ireland from the potent working-class community of the rest of the United Kingdom, and placing them as it were upon the same footing as the exploited but alien Boer –

Connolly Aye, or the Hindoo – or the rebellious Chinese Boxer –

Keir Hardie (*turns to face* CONNOLLY, *and indicates his own cloth cap*) This hat, I'd have ye know, was the first true workman's roof ever to have been seen proceeding into the portals of the House of Commons. You can match that, you can answer me: if not, you'd best bide quiet . . . So . . .

Labour in parliament can only achieve anything if part of its programme is adopted by the Liberals who in turn are dependent upon the votes of the Irish Party. The Irish Party demand that the Liberals, when in office, bring in a bill for Home Rule. QED – Labour must give support to Home Rule. Indeed we would prefer in the long run an Irish Republic, but –

Connolly D'ye think we could have that in writing, Mr Keir Hardie?

Keir Hardie The long run being not before we have built a majority party of our own. The recent results of the municipal elections have proved that the basic desires of the Irish working class, as expressed through the ballot-box –

Connolly Forty per cent of the adult males cannot vote – and that forty per cent are entirely working class.

Keir Hardie The basic desires of the Irish working class have nothing whatever to do with the dream of a republic! Municipal administration – gas-board, water-board, housing – as already in large measure achieved in protestant Belfast – and of course the development of trades unions in industry. Until you are prepared to devote your energies to that, the policy of the Independent Labour Party of Great Britain – I am sorry, but there's no help for it, it's a matter of common sense – will be to co-operate and to consult upon Irish affairs with the Irish Parliamentary Party under the leadership of John Redmond.

Grabitall (*sings*)
> Crookey and O'Hookey shake on that
> It is indeed a feather in their hat –
> (Exchanges the hat)

A general swap-around of hats, between GRABITALL, *the* EMPLOYERS *and* KEIR HARDIE. *The latter has been approached by the* EMPLOYERS *from behind, and induced to shake hands. At the end of the hat-changes* KEIR HARDIE'*s cap is on* GRABITALL'*s head,* GRABITALL'*s topper on* KEIR HARDIE, *and the two* EMPLOYERS' *hats are mutually exchanged . . .*

1st Employer (*sings*)
> That our friends across the water –

2nd Employer (*sings*)
> Lead their own friends to the slaughter –

Grabitall and Employers (*sing*)
> And our profits are safeguarded, tit-for-tat!

HARDIE *discovers what he is wearing and indignantly swaps back again with* GRABITALL. *He turns his back on the trio.*

Keir Hardie (*to Connolly*) I'm afraid your socialism in Ireland is up the creek both oar and paddle: Jim, pull yourself to the ground, man, before you're blown beyond the moon!

Connolly I demand an opportunity to make a full and reasoned reply to this disastrous misjudgement –

Keir Hardie Get some votes in, laddie, and then we'll listen. I'm not interested in piss-and-wind . . .!

Exit KEIR HARDIE.

SCENE 12

CONNOLLY *suddenly leaps off the stage and runs up and down among the audience shouting.*

Connolly I will not be dictated to! Victory for the Boers and an Irish Republic – Victory for the Boers and an Irish Republic – Victory for the Boers and an Irish Republic – !

GRABITALL *sends the* POLICE OFFICER *to try and catch him. There is a chase: but* CONNOLLY'*s cry is taken up by a crowd of people who come in and all mill about yelling. Finally* CONNOLLY *leaves the hall, with his supporters, still to be heard shouting offstage.*

Grabitall (*to* EMPLOYERS)
    Crookey – O'Hookey – ! – a job – a job
    Contrived to drown the deafening of this mob!

The crowd comes in on the stage and this time chases GRABITALL *who runs about for a while. Finally he leaves them behind and re-enters on stage to the cowering* EMPLOYERS.

    They're after you, you know, as well as me!
    So, save yourselves by putting in your plea . . .?
    I say save yourselves by putting in your plea!

The EMPLOYERS *for a moment are nonplussed.*

3rd Employer (*gets it*)
    I have it, sorr, I take your drift – why don't we all invite the Duke of York?
1st Employer Too small at all at all – he didn't work . . .
3rd Employer Ah sure, what's the Duke of York?
1st Employer A little whipper-snapper of a diffident grandson that couldn't say boo to a goose – no no, sorr, 'tis inevitable –
3rd Employer Sure, it can't be delayed any longer –
1st Employer The old lady!
3rd Employer The old lady!
1st Employer We must have in the old lady!

Employers Sure, nothing will go wrong.

Grabitall Fill the town with loyal protestants from Harland and Wolff of Belfast – all the school children get a holiday and be marshalled with their teachers – the Lord Lieutenant will provide them with a treat in the afternoon. The employees of Guinness's brewery will get a holiday and a shilling bonus, and be marshalled, with their supervisors. Civil servants –

3rd Employer And their wives –

Grabitall Soldiers off duty –

1st Employer And their wives –

3rd Employer Policemen –

Grabitall Castle officials –

3rd Employer Military pensioners –

Grabitall And their wives. – The wives will bring the children, and the children will be given flags . . .

A loyal crowd assembles and are given union jacks to wave. POLICE *assemble in large numbers.*

Are we ready?

CONNOLLY *appears at a distant corner.*

Connolly Monarchy is a survival of the tyranny imposed by the hand of greed and treachery in the darkest and most ignorant days of our history –

Grabitall We can't have that!

GRIFFITH *appears at another corner.*

Griffith The Famine Queen of England, had she had her way, would have starved every Irishman out of this world in eighteen forty-seven – she is nothing more than a living symbol of the permanent hatred felt by the dull Teuton for the free poetic Gael –

Grabitall The police must take action!

Police Officer What sort of action?

Grabitall By no means the same sort as you took for Joe Chamberlain and even less for the Duke of York! Just keep them off the streets. I said fill the streets with children. I don't see any children!

Police Officer If you please, sir, there appear to be no children to be found . . .

MAUD GONNE *enters, leading a file of children.*

Maud Gonne (*sings*)
      O all you little children come follow after me
      And in honour of your native land I will give you cake and tea:
      Don't go with the Lord Lieutenant: don't go up to Phoenix Park –
      He will put you in his big black pot for his dinner in the dark.

> Come with me, come with me, where the shamrock leaves are
> green
> I will save you from the dragon teeth of the hungry Famine
> Queen . . .

She leads the children round the house and out.

Grabitall (*to* POLICE, *who are about to chase her*) No, stay where you are, we
haven't got time! Cross your fingers, touch wood, say a prayer – we've
got to go through with it! Bring on the Queen of England!

Connolly (*shouts above the cheers and music*) The mind accustomed to political
kings can too easily be reconciled to social kings – capitalist kings of the
workshop, the mill, the shipyard and the docks . . .

To the tune of 'God Save The Queen', a puppet representing QUEEN VIC-
TORIA *is trundled across the stage before the excited crowd.* GRIFFITH *and*
CONNOLLY *come running down towards her – both of them are struck simul-
taneously to the ground by police batons.*

Grabitall Now get her back to England – quick!

The QUEEN *is hurried out and the crowd disperses.*

> Nobody in Ireland, from now on, is going to be allowed to do anything
> at all – if I don't like the look of it! Enforce that at once!

Police Officer Yessir, at once, sir! Where shall we start, sir?

Grabitall (*indicates* GRIFFITH) With him. Seize his newspaper.

Police Officer Smash up his printing press?

Grabitall We do not want to start another riot!
> Our only purpose now is keep things quiet.
> Forbid all public meeting and procession.

Police Officer
> That ban will be broken.

Enter CIVIL SERVANT, *with newspapers.*

Civil Servant
> No – no – it won't! The stock exchange has spoken!
> *The Wall Street Journal* and the London *Times* –
> 'Severe depression
> Affecting trade and all employment – !'

Grabitall Saved! We are saved! At the very last moment!
> But yet we must make haste to circumvent
> Trade union opposition to our firm-principled intent.
> The employer here pays off a very old grudge,
> Assisted by his friend, the high court judge . . .

SCENE 13

A JUDGE *in his wig and robes comes in.*

Judge 'Quin versus Leatham . . .'
Grabitall An Irish lawsuit started in Belfast:
    Most salutory that Ireland should come first.
    And after – to South Wales:
    No trains upon the rails –
    Judgement, if you please, before the company should fail!
Judge 'The Taff Vale Railway versus the Amalgamated Society of Railway
Servants . . .' In both of these cases the judgement is as follows: trade
unions are held liable for all damages and loss incurred by industrial
action. So therefore the man Quin, and his so-called Butchers' Union,
must pay to Mr Leatham, a slaughterhouse proprietor, the sum of two
hundred and fifty pounds: while the Amalgamated Society of Railway
Servants must pay the Taff Vale Railway no less than forty thousand.
That will teach them to withdraw their labour upon the whim of a fanciful
grievance and hold the whole community to unauthorised ransom.
Grabitall If the unions are left
    Without a penny to their name
    They have none but themselves to blame.
    There is nothing they can do –
    But pay the bill –
Judge And pay the lawyers, too!
Grabitall We'll find their money-bags from now not quite so full
    Of proud disruption and democracy abused.
    Prices will rise, wages will fall:
    With no-one permitted to do anything at all,
    Nothing will happen. People will be so confused
    The very vote itself will not be used.
    Unless in favour of Conservative . . .
    For when a man can hardly stay alive,
    What greater blessing can he know
    Than to conserve the status quo?
    Hungry folk are rarely over-bold:
    Rather than starve, they do what they are told!

    Exeunt all but CONNOLLY.

Connolly (*gets slowly to his feet and addresses the audience*)
    I would prefer to prove him wrong.
    We filled the streets and sang our song:
    We thought we heard ourselves applauded.
    Our short sharp entertainment is concluded –
    Those we thought

Joined in with us on every note
In fact throughout
We now so ruefully can have no doubt
Had kept their mouths tight shut . . .

Exit.

END OF ACT 2

ACT 3: 'Outmanoeuvred'

SCENE 1

Converging processions of demonstrators representing socialist and nationalist ferment from different parts of the world, in a variety of costumes and with a variety of slogans on their banners in many languages. The whole contained within a border of watchful police of no particular nationality. (Backcloth 5.)

Enter CONNOLLY, *very depressed, and an* OLD MARKET-WOMAN *with a basket of Christmas holly, etc., to sell.*

Connolly (*sings*)
> For weeks and months I've been so tormented
> With agitation for the public weal –
> Blood in my face and my bold brain beating
> Against the base of my angry skull.
>
> I have had no time for wife nor family
> I have had no time to speak a civil word
> To friend nor neighbour – like a wild red Indian
> I have prowled through the town without sleep or food.
>
> I am hardly aware of the date or the day of it –
> What is the month . . . ?

Old Market-Woman
> December.

Connolly (*sings*)
> What day . . . ?

Old Market-Woman
> It is the twenty-fourth: your chiselurs are expecting you.

Connolly (*sings*)
> Nothing I can bring them, there is nothing I can say . . .

Exit OLD MARKET-WOMAN. *As she goes a bit of greenery falls from her basket.* CONNOLLY *picks it up, is about to call after her, then looks at it – it is only a fragment – he rather guiltily shoves it under his coat. A* BEGGING CHILD *accosts him.*

Begging Child Hey, mister – a merry Christmas – d'ye have a wee penny for us –?

Connolly (*cornered, after he tries in vain to hurry past*) Aye . . . merry Christmas. But I'm afraid I've got no penny.

Begging Child Please, mister, please – me da broke his leg and there's nothing in the house and me mammy said –

Connolly Nothing?

Begging Child Me mammy said I was to go out and ask for pennies in the market or else there would be nothing.

Connolly Here – here's a ha'penny – no, wait a minute, I can just make it two – here's three ha'pennies and that's all.

The BEGGING CHILD *scampers away.*

In my own house, what will there be?

He sings:

> On Christmas eve, in a house without festivity
> Where is the pudding should be boiling in the pan?
> Christmas eve and no money in my pocket –

SCENE 2

CONNOLLY *arrives home and* LILLIE *and* NORA *greet him.*

Connolly (*sings*)

> But two shillings for a gift, Lillie, spend them how you can . . .
>
> It is not that I forgot, Lillie . . . but . . . No: do you see these!

Out of his pedlar's pack he takes a suddenly remembered bit of coloured and gilt ribbon.

I sold two of them in two days and one of them was charged to credit.

Lillie James, do you really think you ought to accept credit?

Connolly There was ten children in that tenement and the father in Mountjoy gaol . . . Hang them up for us – on the tree.

Lillie Do you know that in Moore Street they were charging a whole half-crown for a splinter of wood and a splutter of branches like a brush you'd use to sweep the chimney? So you see: there's no tree.

CONNOLLY *looks grave, shakes his head: then suddenly as though by magic whips the bit of green stuff from out behind him.*

Connolly (*sings*)

> Ding-dong merrily on high
> In heaven the bells are ringing
> Ding-dong merrily on high
> On earth the quires are singing –
> Gloria in excelsis!

Put it up on the mantle-piece, put the gew-gaws on it: so!

His improvisation is received with great excitement and delight.

There ye are then, that's a tree!

Lillie For behold I bring you good tidings of great joy which shall be unto all people . . .

Connolly As for that, we do have the newspaper being printed once again. No subscriptions – or hardly any.

Lillie For ourselves to have nothing, there must be others who have far less.

Connolly And is that a consolation . . .? Lillie, what's less than nothing?

Lillie Now, James, in front of the children . . .

Connolly All right: let them answer. Nora, what's less than nothing?

Nora Less than nothing would be if Daddy had forgotten to pick up a branch from the gutter.

Lillie Less than nothing is to have nothing and no way of knowing why, and no comprehension as to how things might be changed. You gave me that comprehension. You have given it to many others.

Connolly Many others? A few others. One or two: no more than that.

Lillie In the old days, in Edinburgh, you were a big success – as a lecturer, I mean.

Connolly Better audiences than I've ever had in this reproachful country.

Lillie Had you not best go back again?

Connolly What? All of us? The whole family – and you yet once more with a baby on the way? Lillie, are you mad?

Lillie No, of course not the whole family. But you are well enough known now to get engagements to lecture in all manner of places in Scotland and England – all you need do is put an advertisement in one of the socialist newspapers – surely that is not going to cost us more than two bob? Go on now, go and do it.

Connolly And leave you here alone? Lillie, that is not a risk I am at all inclined to take. God knows what could happen – suppose I fell ill in England, or the fees for the lectures never came through – or the children were ill or an accident – and besides, in this neighbourhood: it's a very rough area for a mother without a husband – and the conditions of these houses –

Lillie I had words with the rent-collector on that subject yesterday.

Connolly Aye?

Lillie I pointed out to him the hole in the tread of the staircase just below our landing – I said any child could catch her foot in that without thinking: and then himself and his master the landlord would have a death on their hands.

Connolly And he said . . .?

Lillie He said 'Missus – you already have an *agitator* on *your* hands' – he meant you – he said I ought to think meself lucky to be allowed to stay in the place at all, the way the newspapers put names on you when you rose up against the Queen's visit.

Connolly That's exactly what I mean – with me here, they're afraid of me, but if I were to go to England –

SCENE 3

Enter a NEIGHBOUR.

Neighbour Oh – excuse me – Mrs Connolly – is your husband at home?

Connolly Why, hello, Mr Riordan – come in, sir. A merry Christmas to you, Mr Riordan! Lillie, have we got anything we could offer to Mr Riordan to –

He makes a drinking gesture to LILLIE, *who shakes her head, embarrassed.*

Neighbour Oh don't trouble yourself at all, Mr Connolly, sure I only put me head in on me way home from work, being asked to deliver a small message if it's quite convenient . . .

Connolly Yes, yes . . . by all means . . .

Neighbour It's the tenants, Mr Connolly, in O'Sullivan's Buildings, you know the place – in the Coombe? Well me sister's husband Terry is a member of the committee they're after forming over there to defend themselves against eviction – there was th'increase, y'see, of rent: and sure to God they can't pay it: so they made up their minds to resist –

Connolly They did!

Neighbour They did so, sir.

Connolly Good for them. Can I help?

Neighbour Sure wasn't that the very message? They have a meeting in the square the evening after St Stephen's, and they wanted to know, if it was altogether convenient, would you be so good as to address them, Mr Connolly? It would help them a power of good, sir, if they had a speaker like yourself; one of their own, as it were, that could advise them and they could trust . . .

Connolly Mr Riordan, tell the brother-in-law I shall be only too happy to come!

Neighbour Mr Connolly, thank you. You're a good man in time of trouble.

Exit NEIGHBOUR.

Lillie Was that wise?

Connolly If we're in queer street with our own landlord it certainly is a bit of a risk, but –

Lillie But it's a risk you are inclined to take . . .? But take the other one, as well. James, you need new places, you need new people –

Connolly And above all we need some cash.
    We filled the streets, we sang our song:
    We thought we heard ourselves applauded . . .
    Dublin it seems is dead, or deaf – I cannot push
    A tune into the drums of ears that will not ring – !
    No doubt my music must be made elsewhere.
    What shall I play? I will declare

The one tune needful for the present day:
True revolution is the enemy of reform!

Lillie Every time you say that, James, I think of meself out shopping: and I
wonder is it true or false, half a loaf better or worse than no bread?

Connolly For little more than half a loaf of bread
The open razor shaved great Samson's head
Clean to the bone till all his strength had fled.
We need to pull both tower and temple down –
Our hair of power must be full-grown:
In Scotland and in England I will tell them so –

Enter TOM LYNG.

Lyng (*holds out a letter*)
To Paris, France, you must prepare to go!
The International Socialist Conference have written to invite
Our party, on its own, to send a delegate –

Connolly Ireland is recognised in her own right
Apart from Britain, at this conference?
For the first time ever our true historic place
By socialists is granted us in the face
Of all the world . . . ? God, Tom, for this alone we're still alive!

Tom Lyng
Here is the letter. It seems to say
That if we go we must pay our own way . . .

Connolly That rules out me, I am afraid . . .
Yourself and Stewart, though, could afford
Your third-class passage and your bed and board?
I'll brief you briefly – 'Revolution or Reform':
That is the theme that takes this conference by storm!

SCENE 4

LILLIE *and* NORA *go out;* CONNOLLY *walks up and down instructing* TOM
LYNG. STEWART *comes in and joins them.*

Connolly The French Socialist Party is split down the middle: one of their
members has accepted a seat in the bourgeois liberal government, which
also includes the notorious General Gallifet – the man who is known as
'The Butcher of the Commune', for the cruelty with which he put down
the great Paris rising of eighteen seventy-one. The justification? They
have at least one socialist in a place of power . . . he will be able, if he is
lucky, to carry out a few reforms. So, little by little, revolution, and its
inconvenience, will be rendered unnecessary . . . Do you need me to tell
you why this must be opposed? To the extent, if it goes so far, of ap-

parently entirely wrecking the international socialist movement . . .?
Consider the possibility of an Irish delegation, for the first time ever at
such a conference, making its weight felt, where it is needed, in the condemnation of these French hypocrites. If we are able to do that, then
perhaps we may be able to avert the day in Ireland, when the same thing
happens here – in my worst dreams I can foresee how our children and
our childrens' children will awake to discover a party of the working
class has joined, without protest, in an independent Irish government
composed of every gombeen man and grabitall-financier from Killiney
to the Hill of Howth! On your way, lads, do your best.

CONNOLLY *retires to one side of the stage. A large red banner reading
'Paris Conference Socialist International 1900' is brought in at the back:
and the stage fills with* DELEGATES, *squabbling and hurling abuse at each
other.* GRABITALL *strides amongst them, dividing them almost by force, so
that they fall back into two clumps. The conference* CHAIRMAN, *equipped
with a speaker's desk in the middle, beats with his gavel for silence.*

Grabitall This five feet that I pace across the floor will separate
Fraternal comradeship from intestinal hate –
Each individual socialist delegate
According to ideology takes his stand
Splitting the vote of nearly every several land –
Upon my right-hand –
French Delegate (*right-wing*)
France!
Grabitall Upon my left-hand!
French Delegate (*left-wing*)
France!
Grabitall Throw down the biting bones, my boys, and make them dance!
Connolly Application from the French left for a vote of condemnation against
the action of the French right in permitting their associate Millerand to
take his seat in the bourgeois government.
French Delegate (*left-wing*) They are renegades – expel them from the move-
ment! Revolution!
Grabitall (*who has now gone to the opposite side of the stage from* CONNOLLY)
Justification by the French right of their attitude towards Millerand.
French Delegate (*right-wing*) Millerand is the first French socialist ever to be
awarded a ministerial portfolio. He is the foot in the door, the spark in
the dry haystack, the spout of water from the rock in the middle of the
desert. Fellow-delegates, we must all welcome the opening of a new
chapter in the reform of social policies!

Uproar

Connolly If the Chairman cannot decide who to call upon next, there may
never be another speaker – ever –

Grabitall He looks around to catch a rescuing eye – ha-ha he is there:
      Distinguished comrade Kautsky, intellectual heir
      Of mighty Marx and Engels, he will dare
      To peer round this obstructed corner . . . With jesuitical device
      Each simple word he speaks, he will interpret twice or thrice . . .
Kautsky Comrades: let us examine very very carefully the exceedingly complex ramifications of this profoundly important crux . . .
Connolly Like wool upon a spindle
      He winds and winds his argument:
      It is all a kind of a swindle –
      But this is comrade Kautsky's bent.
      He approaches his conclusion, he is now about to ask
      The delegates to help him define their collective task . . .
Kautsky (*who has been speaking inaudibly with baroque gestures*) . . . so I offer to this conference the question whether or not it is our historic collective task to resolve the contradictions and obtain a correct compromise . . . ?

The IRISH DELEGATES *are in the body of the hall, to one side.*

Stewart Now that's not what Jim Connolly told us.
Tom Lyng Jim Connolly said – make our weight felt.
Stewart (*as* KAUTSKY *goes on and on*) I don't see how we can argue with a continental of that class. By God, the man's a polymath. I tell you, he scares me rigid . . .
Grabitall Comrade Kautsky's dialectic has already probed so deep
      That two-thirds of the assembly have fallen fast asleep.
Connolly The longer he keeps them stupefied, the more certain it will be
      When he reaches his conclusion, they can do nothing but agree.
Kautsky May I suggest, therefore, fellow-delegates, that we do not *condemn* the French Socialist Party: nor, fellow-delegates, do we make the crucial error of *supporting* their procedure. We consider, very carefully, whether or no the French party were actually *responsible* for the elevation of Millerand to the cabinet of France. I cannot find, upon studying the documents in this case, that at any time were they consulted. The party, as a party, had nothing to do with it. So: the resolution before this conference should, in my opinion, read as follows: 'We criticise the individualist action of comrade Millerand, and recommend the French Socialist Party to impose in the future a more precise discipline.' Do we not think that solves everything . . . ?
Rosa Luxemburg (*jumps up in the body of the hall*) You deliberately evade the entire point that is at issue! We exist here for one purpose: to overthrow capitalism. To tinker with it in the shape of reactionary coalitions is objectively to offer it our support! Whether or not Millerand consulted the French party has nothing at all to do with it. Members of his own party in this hall have defended his action and have called on us to welcome it. Therefore they deserve to be utterly condemned and expelled

from the International. To offer them this compromise for the sake of reuniting their very properly divided party is in itself a blatant gesture of approval towards Millerand!

Chairman Delegates will only speak, please, when called upon by the chair. And we require those who speak from the body of the hall to state their names and affiliations as a preface to their remarks.

Rosa Luxemburg Rosa Luxemburg, member of the German Social Democrats.

Grabitall From the party of comrade Kautsky . . . Yet another group with a split in it!

Connolly Comrade Kautsky is aware of her – and of the book that she has written –

Kautsky *Reform or Revolution* was the title, was it not . . . ? We are all of us beholden to the erudition of comrade Luxemburg. But in matters of practicality she has perhaps a little to learn. She comes, I understand, from Poland, where the tradition has not always been to put all things in their proper order . . .

Tom Lyng Seems to me she's put it very much in the proper order.

Stewart Keep your eye upon her, so: when she votes, we vote with her. Why, she speaks with the very voice of Jim Connolly himself.

Chairman Votes. Those in favour of comrade Kautsky's ingenious compromise?

Grabitall Austria . . . Great Britain . . . Germany . . .

Tom Lyng Why dammit, she doesn't have a vote! She's not an accredited delegate.

Stewart She didn't have the right to put in her opinion at all! But she put it – she's a great girl!

Chairman Those opposed to comrade Kautsky's ingenious compromise?

Polish Delegate (*right-wing*) One moment please! The Polish delegation is unable to reach agreement within itself as to which way it intends to vote! The debate must continue until all delegations have reached unanimity!

Polish Delegate (*left-wing*) By no means! I demand the right to have my dissenting opinion recorded. He wants to vote *for*: I am against! I will never never never be unanimous with him!

Chairman Delegations that are divided will be recorded as such. Those divided?

Grabitall America . . . Italy . . . Poland.

Chairman Finally: those opposed.

Connolly Bulgaria.

Grabitall That's all.

Connolly No no –
Observe: the Irish are standing for the count!
My delegates have their own interpretation of the point . . .

Tom Lyng (*up at the centre of the platform*)
We in Ireland know our Millerand, who he might well be:

The socialist whom Keir Hardie longs to see
Clasping the hand of Redmond and Home Rule!
If we should follow him, our entire life's work would fail.

Grabitall The point is made, but yet it is not taken.
Provincial Irish slogans are not spoken
In such a cosmopolitan atmosphere
Unless you want to get a frozen stare
Of scandalised incomprehension.
Poor Lyng regrets his vulgar intervention . . .

Chairman Delegates voting should refrain please from any comment upon their vote. The debate has been closed.

Bulgarian Delegate No no, excuse me, upon a point of order, comrade chairman: Gromek, Bulgaria. The question already raised by the Polish delegation. If a delegation is divided and has recorded itself as such: then how can this conference recognise both factions of that delegation as truly representative of the country that has sponsored it? For instance – who is Poland? That gentleman: or that one?

Rosa Luxemburg Does it matter?

General cries: 'Of course it matters!'

Rosa Luxemburg (*gets up on to the platform despite the* CHAIRMAN) At an international socialist conference it is important whether *Poland* is truly represented by him – or by him – ? Nonsense! What do we suppose Poland – as a concept – has to do with scientific socialism, which extends beyond frontiers and recognises only *classes* as the fundamental structure of the present state of the human race? Why, Poland, as a concept, does not even exist! The nation, as we all well know, is divided out and ruled by Germany, Austria, Russia, as subordinate provinces of their three respective empires. Why else have I come here as a member of a *German* party?

Stewart Now wait a moment: I've come here as a member of an *Irish* party! By your argument, ma'am, 'tis the *British* delegation that my friend and meself had ought to be attached to?

Rosa Luxemburg That is so: yes.

Tom Lyng But – but – but here, wait a moment – it's for that very reason that we voted against Kautsky!

Rosa Luxemburg I hope not. If you think that revolution can best triumph over reformism by invoking these national differences, then let me caution you both to examine your position. . . .

Grabitall The chairman calls for order: the digression is cut short:
The conference adjourns: the Irish delegates feel quite hurt.

Exeunt all save STEWART, TOM LYNG, *and* ROSA LUXEMBURG: CONNOLLY *stays at the extreme side of the stage, and* GRABITALL *busies himself con-*

temptuously clearing up the debris – tearing down and rolling up the banner,
etc.

Tom Lyng (*catches* ROSA LUXEMBURG *as she makes to go out*) Excuse me,
ma'am: ye have us both extremely bothered.

Stewart We feel obliged to take you up on the things that you said just now.

Tom Lyng Our party is republican, you see: the complete separation of Ireland
from Great Britain is an essential part of our – –

Rosa Luxemburg And so it is with many of the Poles. We have our own
socialists who cling to a utopian and fantastic plan for the reconstitution
of the country. But is not this dangerous heresy, comrades, exactly what
we struggle against? We who are convinced that the proletariat is not in
a position to change political geography, nor to reconstruct bourgeois
states, but that it must organise itself on existing foundations, historically
created, so as to bring about the conquest of socialist power and the
ultimate socialist republic, which alone will be able to liberate the entire
world! *There* should be the true meaning of this word you use – republican.

Stewart Sure she talks like an Orangeman out of Belfast . . . I've heard the
very same argument put forward by labour organisers in the North who
are after nothing more than the supremacy of their own religious sect
over everyone else in the province!

Rosa Luxemburg Ah, religion . . . ! It goes hand-in-hand with national sentiment, as always! Why, christianity and socialism have nothing in common. The subordination of the material welfare of mankind to the will
of the supreme deity . . . ? No no: keep well away from it . . . Do not think
of yourselves as catholics, nor of others as protestants, nor of any of you
as Irishmen: you are proletarians or you are nothing: and your interests
are identical. And let me add: that to set one so-called national interest
in competition against another – in itself, you will observe, a capitalist
activity – inevitably involves militarism: the greatest danger of the
present age. The powers of Europe are expending twenty per cent, thirty
per cent more of their national budget upon armaments than was the
case five years ago. The man who is half a nationalist will always join a
national army when his patriotism is invoked. Remember that . . . But
you did well, in your vote against Kautsky.

Tom Lyng And you did well, yourself, ma'am, in your interruption of that
feller. Congratulations, comrade.

ROSA LUXEMBURG *shakes hands with them and goes out.*

Grabitall Not a little bewildered, they come home, they see their chief:
　　　Do we suppose he can resolve for them the confusion of their belief?

Exit GRABITALL. CONNOLLY *comes to meet* TOM LYNG *and* STEWART.

Connolly You don't want to take too much notice of that Luxemburg one. On reformism, from what you tell me, she's very sound. But as regards the national question: don't forget she's a Pole, and Poland at one time had an empire itself. Did ye never hear of a king of theirs called John Sobiesky? Conquered left right and centre. She's quite right, if she doesn't want any more o' *that* coming up ... She's also, I believe, a Jew: and the Jews have been persecuted the way you'd hunt rabbits by both the Poles and the Russians. So you wouldn't expect the girl to be particularly concerned which one of the two gangs was in charge – if anything she prefers Germany where the Jews have no problems: fellow-citizens with their own religion and no nonsense about it. In her place, quite clearly, national sentiment is of small value: but the Irish question's different and we judge it by different rules. The next time we go to one of these international affairs, we are going to have to work out much more thoroughly our particular philosophy and explain it with great care. But there's time for it. The important thing is: we made a principled stand. And they know now who we are. In due course they'll know us better ...

Exeunt TOM LYNG *and* STEWART.

SCENE 5

Connolly Through the years of nineteen hundred and nineteen hundred and
        one
        It seemed that my travels would never be done.
        Around Scotland and England, east and west
        In third-class carriages without any rest,
        Cheap temperance hotels with damp and cranky beds,
        Audiences in draughty halls invariably at odds:
        And myself on the platform trying to explain to their grotesque
        heads
        The complex clarity of the clear-cut world I dreamed I could
        foresee ...
        I must forbid myself to think that they are bigger fools than me ...

And yet in the name of God what else must I call them ... ? Shall we take for an example this ridiculous Kautsky compromise – the British socialists in Paris voted for it to a man: and yet, in their newspapers, they turn around and abuse Millerand! In Glasgow and Falkirk, Aberdeen, Leith, Salford – inevitably at every lecture I give, it comes up – and inevitably I prepare for it. ...

        Shall I show you how it goes each weary day:
        It always goes the self-same way ...

I dismount from the railway-train, I am met upon the station platform by the inevitably serious young man ... 'Comrade Connolly? How d'ye do, sir, I'm so glad you were able to come – now I can't honestly tell you we expect a *huge* meeting tonight, unexpectedly the date has coincided with the all-in wrestling at the Municipal Free Trade Hall – ha ha – but we have managed to secure for your lecture the Saxe-Coburg Terrace Unitarian Meeting-Rooms, no it's not actually in the *church*, round the back down this small passage-way, through the wicket-gate, mind the step . . . oh dear, I'm afraid the lamp's broken – let's hope the old care-taker hasn't forgotten to leave the key in the thing-a-majig! Aha, here we are! I feel highly confident that those who have prevailed upon themselves to turn up will be a really keen and interested, indeed I might say *devoted* section of the socialist movement in this area – not perhaps entirely *representative* – but we couldn't really expect that, could we, with the situation . . . I mean, socialist politics these days look pretty thin and feeble when our lads at the Boer War are pouring out their hearts' blood for the cause of the cash-nexus. I predict you are going to get a fair amount of heavy questioning on *that* score tonight – but you won't mind . . . ?' And Jasus but he's not wrong! So size up the audience. Launch into it, keep it cool, keep it logical, try to anticipate all objections in the body of the discourse, so that heckling towards the end will find little to take hold of . . . There we are, forty minutes' worth: thank you very much, ladies and gentlemen . . . 'I'm sure if any member of the audience has any questions the speaker would be only too happy to . . .' Wait for it. Here it comes. Number one, from the far left. There's some-one who's been reading something starts quoting Rosa Luxemburg. Irish national aspirations, how to reconcile with socialism.

> Pat-a-cake, pat-a-cake baker's man:
> I've rolled him and wrapped him and put *him* in the pan . . .

No great difficulty so far. Number two, from towards the centre . . . 'Can the speaker explain please how an Independent Labour Party can be expected to function entirely free from all Liberal ties, when the trade union movement is presently hamstrung by the Taff Vale legal judge-ment?' That's a wee bit more complicated. I try to explain that so long as the Liberals remain confident of the Labour vote in parliament, so long will they deliberately delay any action upon Taff Vale – we are therefore dependent for our very political existence upon paying blackmail to our masters. If there's Irish in the audience, I can work a way round this one: for the Liberals are as bound to the Irish Party as Labour is to the Liberals and the answer must clearly be for the Irish voters to transfer support from the Liberal Home Rule policy to Labour and republican-ism – 'ah but, comrade, the British Labour Party is in no way republican' – so make it so, you have the numbers, you have the voice, you have the power – all you lack is the bloody will!

> I've to remember meself damn quick
> Before I call him a stupid Mick:

Watch it, Connolly, watch it, you're going over the brink:
You once start abusing them and by God, boy, you are sunk!
Nearly done, look at my watch,
Ten more minutes and my train to catch –

God, here it comes: Number three from the pig-ignorant right – 'How can you justify your pro-Boer stance?' Fairly polite – before I can answer – 'Pro-Boers is bloody murderers, my brother is shot dead these three weeks in the Argyll and Sutherland Highlanders!' Hold it – where's the chairman – this looks like a put-up job . . .! 'Treason' they shout, 'What about Ladysmith! What about Mafeking! Fucking foreigner get home to where you fucking well came from!' . . . Oh certainly not every night: not inevitable: just often enough to make me nervous as a kitten. At Oxford the undergraduates threw stones at me and drove me out. Oh I went for them and no mistake with the broken handle of the old red banner –

Four of them I laid out flat
But they knocked off me my one good hat –
So much is the worth of a university education
To men who defend the backbone of the great British nation . . .

And oh such confusion about what the British nation even *is*! The Irish Socialist Republican Party must set up branches in Britain: thank God I am not altogether without success at this . . . so far so good. But where-ever and upon what issue, it always boils down to the same old perennial – half-a-loaf-or-no-bread – Aye, it's not only the whole loaf we are demanding but the entire baker's shop! And I warn you it is more than stones will be fired at you to keep you out of it – they'll throw *loaves*! You don't eat them . . . throw them back!

And every day upon the train or in the station waiting-room
I sit huddled in my overcoat and I write my letters home . . .
Money and love for my family, that comes first:
For the party, instructions – and money – and every week such a
    burst
Of exhortation and suspicion and mistrust,
That when I look over what I've written I am forced
To believe that they will believe that I have taken leave
Of the balance of my intellect:
But what else can they expect?
They barely ever write to me to tell me what they are about –
How the devil am I to know if I do not find out?

For example . . . To Tom Lyng: 'Dear Comrade, The meetings here are awful, the smallest I have had in England. I don't much like the idea you put forward in your last letter about establishing a *drinking club* in the party headquarters . . . Please thank O'Brien for being so helpful to me yet again in the matter of money and clothes: I felt so ashamed about having to ask him, it nearly made me resolve never to go back to Dublin again . . . I am still left completely in the dark about the arrangements for printing the newspaper. Please write to me and tell me these things: it's most important . . . The enclosed article about Kautsky and his relevance to the Home Rule Party, will you print it, if you can, in the next number of *The Workers' Republic?* . . . Ah, yes, thank God, some good news! It is truly splendid to hear that the Union of United Labourers have elected me in my absence to the Dublin Trades Council. Even more that they should be pressing for my personal nomination as a candidate for the city elections. I will certainly accept!' And I did . . .

SCENE 6

Enter GRABITALL.

Connolly Three candidates for socialism and against Home Rule
We put into the field: and truth to tell
My hopes once more were high – the more so, I daresay,
That I myself in person stood forward to display
The full extremity of our doctrine – take or leave.
Grabitall They left.
Connolly I now am told that many would have voted for us if only they
could believe
That others would as well.
But very few were brave enough to tell
Each other this, so therefore they all thought
The party of their choice had no support:
Therefore they placed their votes elsewhere . . .
Grabitall Here is one reason why they did not dare.

Enter a PRIEST. (EMPLOYERS *behind him.*)

Priest My dear children, as your parish priest, I inform you that James Connolly is an atheist: and of course, a baptised catholic who willingly and wittingly votes for a known exposed atheist renders himself liable to automatic excommunication.
1st Employer Very much obliged to you, Father . . .
3rd Employer That covers it very nicely . . .

Exeunt GRABITALL, EMPLOYERS *and* PRIEST.

Connolly Four hundred and thirty-one votes may appear to be very small:
In the circumstances, 'tis a wonder I got any at all . . .

SCENE 7

Connolly Nothing for it: turn my back,
Divert across the ocean my zig-zag lonely track –
Drive my furrow to America, the soil there at least is thick:
And that which can be planted may well contrive to grow.
Without I try it out I cannot know.
I go.

The invitation came from Daniel De Leon and the American Socialist Labour Party. They are anxious to have an Irish lecturer to speak
principally to audiences of working-class emigrants: and to convince
them that the national independence of Ireland is better served by socialism than by the Home Rule nationalist cliques, which already control
large areas of industrial America. Tammany Hall, in fact. Gangsters.
Catholicism and corrupt patronage. Well, there's one thing about
America – whatever your politics, they are stark mad about public lectures!

Enter an American CHORUS-LINE (*men in bow-ties and flat straw hats, with
canes: girls in fishnet tights with bunches of feathers on their buttocks: one
man representing a* RAILWAY-CONDUCTOR *with a peaked cap, a whistle to
blow, and a flag.*) *They dance a routine in the manner of a travelling train,
stopping between the stanzas of the song.* CONNOLLY, *with a battered suit-
case and his lecture notes, trots along with the dancers, miming speeches at
each pause: gradually becoming more and more exhausted.*

Conductor (*sings*)
From New York State via Salt Lake City
To San Francisco Bay
This is no trip that a man can take
In a matter of a night and a day.
Chorus (*sings*)
Oh the wheels they spin and the train-bells ring
And the engines blow and blow
Across the plain and over the range
Six months upon the go.
Conductor (*after pause – sings*)
All aboard . . .!
To Yonkers, Tarrytown, Boston, Buffalo,
Minneapolis and St Paul:
This wandering man traversed the land
with his words like a waterfall.
Chorus (*sing*)
Oh the wheels they spin and the train-bells ring
And the engines blow and blow

> Across the plain and over the range
> Six months upon the go.

Conductor (*after pause – sings*)
> All aboard . . .!
> California where the orange groves
> Are ripened into gold
> Colorado where the miners' lives
> Are cruelly bought and sold.

Chorus (*sings*)
> On the wheels they spin and the train-bells ring
> And the engines blow and blow
> Across the plain and over the range
> Six months upon the go.

Conductor (*after pause – sings*)
> All aboard . . .!
> By dark Detroit to the eastern sea
> How the crowds come round and cheer
> Are the rebel hands that built this land
> Now ready to rebel once more?

Connolly (*breaks away from the movement and singing down front as dance goes on behind him*)
> Or the goon and the gun and the lawyer's tongue
> Are they stronger than ever before?
> There is nothing I can do but tell it true
> And hope that someone will hear.

Taken me half a year – I've travelled six thousand miles – and thank God, that wraps it up . . .

The CHORUS *now dances undulating as it might be ship at sea –* CONNOLLY *at the rear waves good-bye to the USA . . .*

Chorus (*sings*)
> Oh the screws they spin and the ship-bells ring
> And the ocean gales do blow
> Astride the tide to the Irish side
> Now homeward I must go . . .

Connolly All that I earned I sent forward before me – so much for Lillie and the children – so much for the newspaper – so much for the general funds of the Party. It will have been well spent.

SCENE 8

Enter O'BRIEN, THE LYNGS, STEWART, *and* BRADSHAWE. *They sit as for a committee meeting: then seeing* CONNOLLY, *they stand and welcome him with a song.*

ISRP (*sings*)
> Here's a welcome to Old Jim
> Far and wide he had to roam
> Oh we missed him when he was gone
> And we're glad to have him home.
>
> Oh we're glad to have him home
> There is so much work to be done
> And the only man to do it
> Is the noble hero Jim!
>
> Notwithstanding we are socialists
> And we work all as a team –
> The success of such a party
> Cannot depend upon one man.
>
> Jim is useful, that's well known
> And we're glad to have him home:
> But we got on very nicely thank you
> All upon our own . . .

Connolly Something's gone wrong. No clue to it in your letters. Tell me.
O'Brien No no, Jim, there's nothing . . .
Jack Lyng (*after a pause*) The Municipal Elections.
Stewart We had to get going with the arrangements on our own.
Tom Lyng We thought we should make a change.
O'Brien We lost heavily last year at Wood Quay.
Connolly Where myself was the candidate.
Stewart We should select a new ward to put up our candidate this time.
Connolly Select a new candidate . . . ?
Tom Lyng Now we didn't say that.
Jack Lyng Tom, you're handling this all wrong. Jim, listen to me, there was never a suggestion whatever that you as candidate should be replaced! But the electorate at Wood Quay –
Stewart Will have nothing to do with us.
Connolly So you suggest we shift our ground? Altogether a novel political principle – the nomadic conception. Very well then: where?
Stewart (*after a pause*) We thought maybe Ringsend.

Another pause. CONNOLLY *gets up and walks away from them, thinking. While his back is turned,* TOM LYNG *does something with a lemonade bottle from which* BRADSHAWE *has been taking refreshment.* STEWART *watches this by-play and he and* TOM LYNG *wink at one another.* CONNOLLY *suddenly turns round on them.*

Connolly Ah! Good! Ringsend. I wonder why?
Tom Lyng There's a good deal of support there –

Connolly There certainly wasn't before I went to America.

Stewart We're after selling a crowd of copies of the newspaper down there –

Connolly And how many is a crowd?

Stewart Harry Brady lets us hawk them to the customers in his bar on a Friday night – I can get rid of a dozen a week there: now I think we should try to be building on that.

Connolly Build votes on twelve copies flogged to drunks who can hardly read? You're out of your mind. Wood Quay or nowhere.

Stewart Look, the publicans and the slum-owners have come together with the clergy to put a very black name upon socialism in Wood Quay. Haven't they threatened to raise up the rents of the tenants if our vote is increased?

Jack Lyng Jim, it's a matter of tactics – we must move into a district where we're not already known –

Connolly Ha, yes, not known? I thought you told me the Ringsend boozers were flooded out with our newspaper?

Stewart There have been no articles in the paper lately attacking the sellers of drink. So long as we can contrive not to antagonise Harry Brady with the class of manifesto you put out last year in Wood Quay, I would imagine that we could have the freedom of his bar –

Connolly Just what in the name of God have you been printing in that paper? Will ye give me at once a copy of the latest edition!

o'BRIEN *hands him a newspaper.*

I read this one in Detroit, six weeks ago. I said the latest –

O'Brien The fact is, that paper there is the last one to come off the press. The fact is, the fact of the matter, there's been a proper financial fuck-up.

Bradshawe (*who has suddenly got drunk*) Fuck-up, says your man. You can't *get* a fucken paper without ye first get your paper to print it on – right? So the stationers won't sell us the fucken paper, nor yet ink. These brainless fucken gawms here, Jim, d'ye realize what they've gone and done? They've put the fucken printing-press – *our* press, belongs to *us* – they've put the fucker into hock to pay the bills of the paper-merchants . . . and yet still the bills aren't paid . . . If I didn't know that I'd never been anything else than a totallyteetotaller . . . I would tell youse stupid bastards that I had got meself fucken drunk . . .

Connolly You had better go home.

BRADSHAWE *staggers out.*

What kind of game have you been playing with this – member?

Tom Lyng Now look, Jim, 'twas no more than a harmless prank of a joke –

Stewart Sick to death of his crawthumping about the evils of drink, that's all . . . A lad that can't tell gin from fizzy lemonade ought not to be in bloody politics.

Connolly (*picks up the lemonade bottle*) I suppose this belongs to Harry Brady.

Stewart Indeed it doesn't – it belongs to us. And there's a deposit on that bottle – you don't just throw it away!

Connolly Deposit? Belongs to us?

Tom Lyng In view of the lack of interest you showed in your letters when I put the project forward, we were compelled to take a decision in response to the situation. Quite normal in societies and clubs of any sort to apply for a beer-and-spirits licence: I mean, for heaven's sake, man, we haven't opened a *saloon* – there's a small cupboard in the back office and we buy the stuff outside and bring it in by the crate.

Connolly Who buys it?

Stewart I do.

Connolly Who from?

Stewart All sorts of places.

Connolly Harry Brady?

Stewart Why not? If he has fair prices?

Connolly It is apparent to me he has very far from fair prices! Because, Jasus, if he had, we would not now be insolvent! And all the money that I earned, through six months in America, would not now be poured away – for what? A licensed bloody bar, a prank of a joke, and a printing-press in hock!

They all sit silent, ashamed.

I shall say and think no more of it. I hope to God you will do likewise. The election will test all. Wood Quay!

Enter GRABITALL.

Grabitall Last year James Connolly got four hundred and thirty-one votes. This year James Connolly gets two hundred and forty-three.
Exit GRABITALL. *The* ISRP MEMBERS *go out, despondent.*

SCENE 9

CONNOLLY *sits at a table and starts writing.*

Connolly James Connolly sat down
      And pen and paper he took
      Without a word he set to work
      Writing his history book.

Enter JACK LYNG.

Jack Lyng Jim: the printers of the newspapers have not yet been paid. And we're going to lose the printing-press for good if we can't pay back the money we were loaned on it. Jim, for God's sake – leave your writing for one moment – Jim, what are we going to do?

Connolly Hold a committee-meeting.

The other members of the ISRP enter – BRADSHAWE *is now sober, and even more self-effacing than before.*

Everyone present? Right. Motion before this meeting: all money in the kitty goes direct towards the payment of outstanding debts incurred by the party-newspaper. All the money. All. Anybody second that . . .? Oh come on: we are a revolutionary political party. Financially we're bankrupt – our organisation is in fragments – and we have nothing whatever to restore ourselves with. Except ideas. Except, comrades, the quality of our political ideas. Those ideas have been permanently expressed on the pages of our newspaper. And also, as you know, in the pages of my half-finished book *Labour in Irish History* which – as you know – has been regularly appearing as a serial in the newspaper. I have my name on the title-page: but only because it is customary. The real author of the book is the Irish Socialist Republican Party. The book, in fact is us: and if we cannot get it printed, our voice has been struck dumb. Add to that the question of reliability and trust. Are you not aware that there are literally hundreds of subscribers in America, who have paid up their money and who expect to receive their copies? Upon what else, therefore, do you suggest that we expend our resources?

O'Brien There's the rent for the committee-room.

Tom Lyng There's a whole lot of expenses that have to be settled first. Oh we've had to put out money out of our own pockets, I'd have you know! Stewart has the list.

Stewart I have here a wee chitty, every penny of it's on it. There was three-and-sixpence for the cardboard for the placards for the picket . . .

Connolly Any reason why ye shouldn't have got your old pal Harry Brady to have *given* you the bloody cardboard? Go on, read the next one.

Stewart The next item's rather large. But we held it to be justified. It's twelve shillings and eightpence – the return fare to Athlone.

Connolly And who was the excursionist?

Tom Lyng Gerry O'Malley.

Connolly Who?

Tom Lyng Ah sure you know Limping Gerry. He helped us out many's the time delivering the leaflets. Of course he's been unable to come forward openly as a member, on account of his brother being a sergeant in the constabulary – but –

Connolly If it's the Limping Gerry *I'm* thinking of, his distribution of leaflets was usually confined to leaving them in a lump in the gentlemen's, for whatever purpose. Why Athlone?

Stewart Didn't his mother want him home for Christmas, and she with a bad leg?

Connolly I thought it was himself was after breaking his leg . . . Read your list.

O'Brien I don't think there's any point. It seems to me you are determined to make mockery and scoff of every piddling bloody thing. You have a motion you have put before this committee. We spend everything we've got upon the publication of your book – or we endeavour to space it out upon regular political needs in a reasonable proportion.

Connolly I did not say *my book*! I said the newspaper . . .!

Stewart Which *is* your book – look at it! There's nothing in it but your book! For God's sake let's have a vote upon the motion of comrade Connolly . . . Those in favour . . .? Hardly any. Those against . . .? Aye, nearly everyone. So what are you going to do?

Connolly Resign.

Jack Lyng Man, you cannot resign!

Connolly Can I not, Jack? Why, I have.

Jack Lyng But we don't have to accept that –

Stewart I propose that this committee should accept the resignation of comrade Connolly forthwith. Those in favour . . .? It's a majority.

The MEMBERS *get up to go.*

O'Brien (*turns back as he goes out*) Jim, when all's said – you did lose two hundred votes . . .

CONNOLLY *is left alone.*

SCENE 10

Connolly Party or no party, I must continue to publish the paper . . .
Why, sure, they will ask me back:
They will beg me to reconsider.

Enter LILLIE.

Lillie James, I think you will have to let them make their own mistakes for a while.

Connolly For ever! By God: I've done with them! If it had been any other issue but the question of the newspaper –

Lillie You said you would continue to publish it yourself . . .?

Connolly How? When? Where? It isn't possible . . . Not in Dublin . . . Suppose, Scotland. Now, here's a point. There's a good man called Matheson. I talked with him in Glasgow about the opportunity to set up a Scottish equivalent to De Leon's Socialist Labour Party. He also suggested that it might not be impracticable to print *The Workers' Republic* over there – what about that? Wait a minute – Lillie – think: I could go to the Edinburgh technical college, and I could take a proper course in linotype operation! Yet – oh confound it – not even Scotland and the socialism in Scotland is capable of a wage to keep me and you and all the children . . .! I imagine, in the entire English-speaking world, De

Leon alone has a socialist party-structure sufficiently large to afford
employment and security to a family man . . . and we do have to think
of that.

Lillie You approve of his party?

Connolly He has a strong, theoretical, permanent nucleus of very well-
disciplined members: when I was over there last year I was enormously
impressed – and their newspaper – it's not just a sheet, you know – it's as
large and as competently produced as *The Irish Times*! You know he as
good as told me if I ever went back to New York I could have a job for the
asking on the editorial board? And failing that, if I learnt the linotype
yoke, why wouldn't I walk straight in and take my place at his printing-
press? Why, in New York, we could live like – I was going to say *kings*
but *Americans* is good enough . . .!

Lillie We?

Connolly Would you not want to come?

Lillie Well, I don't want to stay here!

Connolly Scotland first, get together with Matheson, then from there to New
York, and you follow me as soon as I'm fixed! What are you laughing
at?

Lillie I was just thinking, how many emigrants have set off for America,
weeping and all mournful because they were compelled there by their
landlords – you must be the first one to be driven out by the socialists –
and you're not mournful at all!

Connolly It's not villainy, it's stupidity – oh we can laugh at it, we can plot
revenge!

> Like coals of fire heaped on them head and tail
> When they receive via transatlantic mail
> The newspaper, the pamphlet – and the book
> That I myself will print in 'God's Own Country' – they will look
> At what is written on the title-page: and it will read –
> 'Jim Connolly made this – you had better pay good heed!
> It tells you all you want to know –
> It was his wife, you see, showed him the way to go . . .'
> They'll say – 'Lord save us, I remember him!
> Them Yanks is welcome to the busy Jim.
> Do you suppose we'll ever get him back?'
> Then one of them – O'Brien perhaps – will think a bit
> And slowly answer – 'I am sure of it:
> But when he comes, he will have left behind
> The American-Irish finally of one mind.
> With their political voice, their dollars, they will give aid
> No more to the Home Rule hypocrites nor yet to the futile trade
> Of worn-out Fenian terrorism: but socialist one and all
> They'll rally to the sound republican call

To liberate our nation not alone
From foreign despots but also from our own
Self-generated capitalistic maggots . . .'
Ho – coals of fire, why, dammit, we'll pile up *faggots*!
O'Brien will cry, in midst of the roaring flame:
'To send Jim off, indeed we were to blame;
But how much more to blame would we now be
If he had never travelled across the sea?'
Irish revolution will not come
Unless the Irish in their New World home
Prepare it, foster it, and so send it back:
De Leon is the key to the Dublin Castle lock,
And the hand to force him in, to turn the protesting latch
Is the hand of poor Jim Connolly, whom all men think has met
    his match.

Lillie Holding his wife to his heart
    Awake, alive, defiant,
    He puts forward his feet once more
    In the seven-league boots of a giant.

Enter GRABITALL *as they go out.*

Grabitall He puts forward his feet without fear .
    Good God will he never be taught
    That the world both new and old
    By no-one but me is controlled:
    And when the message comes: 'You're through!' –
    That message, little man, is meant for *you* . . .!

END OF PART THREE

Margaretta D'Arcy and John Arden

The Non-Stop Connolly Show

A Dramatic Cycle of Continuous Struggle in Six Parts

Part One: Boyhood 1868–1889

James Connolly, born among the Irish in Edinburgh, can find no
work, so joins the Army and is sent to Ireland. He discovers
Irish nationalism and international socialism: he discovers a
wife: he discovers his political destiny. He determines to go
elsewhere.

Part Two: Apprenticeship 1889–1896

James Connolly, in Edinburgh once more and married, gains
experience in the pioneer socialist movement. He seeks political
office and fails to find it: he seeks to earn a living and fails
likewise. He determines to go elsewhere.

Part Three: Professional 1896–1903

Act I: A Movement with Some Purpose.
  James Connolly becomes a political organiser in Dublin and
founds the Irish Socialist Republican Party. He meets the New
Ireland of the literary renaissance and disrupts the royal Jubilee.

Act II: Alarums and Excursions.
  James Connolly, in Dublin, leads the Irish Socialist Republican
Party in militant opposition to British imperialism and the Boer
War. He is criticised by Keir Hardie of the British Labour
movement.

Act III: Outmanoeuvred.
  James Connolly is rejoiced to find the Irish Socialist Republican
Party recognised by the Socialist International. Rosa Luxemburg
– in controversy with Kautsky – throws doubt upon Connolly's
views of Irish nationhood. The Irish Socialist Republican Party
throws doubt upon his views of political priorities. He determines
to go elsewhere.

Part Four: The New World 1903–1910

Act I: Into the Party.
> James Connolly emigrates to the United States. He joins the
> Socialist Labor Party, led by Daniel De Leon. He is frustrated
> by its doctrinaire sectarianism.

Act II: Out of the Party.
> James Connolly greets with enthusiasm the Industrial Workers
> of the World, believing them to be the great new revolutionary
> force. He forms the Irish Socialist Federation among immigrants
> in the USA. Unable to accommodate himself to De Leon's
> control of the Socialist Labor Party, he determines to pursue
> his politics elsewhere.

Act III: Forward to the Revolution . . . ?
> James Connolly, as IWW Organiser, struggles against odds in
> New York. He helps the presidential election campaign of
> Eugene Debs. He becomes a paid worker for the Socialist Party
> of America. He determines to go elsewhere.

Part Five: The Great Lockout 1910–1914

Act I: Donnybrook Fair.
> James Connolly returns to Ireland and its furious political and
> trade union confusions. He meets James Larkin, who sends him
> to Belfast to organise the new Irish Transport Workers' Union.
> He has ideological clashes with William Walker of the Northern
> Ireland labour movement.

Act II: Keir Hardie's Promise.
> James Connolly continues his work in Ireland for the labour
> movement. The Irish Labour Party is founded. The Dublin
> Employers' Federation is founded. The 'Great Lockout' is
> imposed: Larkin, aided by Connolly, responds with a general
> strike.

Act III: Once More Go Down To Hell.
> James Connolly sees the Dublin General Strike collapse when
> the British trade union leadership fails to respond to the demands
> of its rank and file that the Irish workers be given positive
> support. The Irish Citizen Army is formed. The Irish National
> Volunteers are formed. The climate of violence intensifies.

Part Six: World War and the Rising 1914–1916

Prologue: King Conaire and the Prohibitions.
    In ancient times good King Conaire saved the country from its
    enemies by fighting them against all odds: even though the
    circumstances of the battle were contrary to the ritual
    prohibitions prescribed by his Druids.

Act I: Clouds of War.
    James Connolly confronts the aftermath of the great lockout in
    Dublin. The Irish constitutional crisis brings fears of civil war,
    combining with the threat of a general strike in Britain.
    International imperial rivalries simultaneously intensify.

Act II: World War to Civil War.
    James Connolly sees international socialism collapse in the face
    of the outbreak of the world war. Resolute in his opposition to
    imperialism in all its forms, he seeks desperately for allies – in
    particular from among the members of the Irish Republican
    Brotherhood within the National Volunteers.

Act III: The Rising.
    James Connolly brings the Irish Citizen Army into the Rising of
    Easter 1916: and thereby becomes the first working-class leader
    to enter the world conflict in the cause of socialism. He is
    compelled to surrender to superior force: and is shot to death.